# THE COLD WAR
# FOR INFORMATION
# TECHNOLOGY
## *The Inside Story*

Janez Škrubej

Strategic Book Publishing and Rights Co.

Strategic Book Publishing and Rights Co.
12620 FM 1960, Suite A4-507
Houston, TX 77065
www.sbpra.com

ISBN: 978-1-61897-835-6

Design: Dedicated Book Services (www.netdbs.com)

# Dedication

# Prologue

Perspectives on the Cold War and information technology will never be the same after this book, written by the president and chief executive officer of Iskra Delta, has been published. The book reveals plots and conspiracies to prevent the development of IT industry companies in Europe because of confrontations between intelligence services. This sounds somewhat conspiratorial today, but given the times, it was normal within the international system of political, business, and intelligence lobbies.

This technological epic of this period of enormous development in the world, which spans the last two decades of the past century, is of major significance. It may serve as incentive to creators of national technological development strategies and to entrepreneurs in a host of information technologies, as well as communications and automation engineering.

Enthusiasm, initiative, perseverance, and commitment to common goals and projects all comprised the unique atmosphere surrounding Iskra Delta employees. Their link at the time with the world's most technologically advanced countries, like Japan and the United States, was excellent, and development- and business-based. English, Japanese, German, Chinese, and Russian languages were spoken fluently by Iskra Delta employees and systematically and mutually cultivated with a high degree of technological and managerial professionalism.

Information technology, IT, remains the top subject of technological domination in the USA and the rest of the world. Its significance is pragmatically linked to possibilities of modeling the human consciousness, its evolution, its system of experience, and, last, with the generation of the meaningful on the highest possible level. Information with meaning requires understanding as a property of the consciousness system, using the circularly perplexed mechanism characterized by syntagma, *the informational—the meaningful—the conscious*. Out of such philosophical substance, the subject called informational consciousness, IC, was under development in the company Iskra Delta Computers (IDC) in 1986. In the strategic, developmental, and engineering oriented environment, this undertaking seemed to be extremely reasonable when looking into the IT future advancement. In 1991, with the appearance of Kurzweil's Spiritual Machines, the technological trends of Iskra Delta were confirmed as a possibility in the framework of company's engineering strategy.

Before 1991, IDC's development and engineering was intensively engaged in microprocessor and multiprocessor equipment, in a conceptually and developmentally original way, for instance, in multiprocessor interconnection networking and basic multiprocessing operating systems. Some details of concepts and integrated hardware and software have been lectured about and demonstrated in IT-concerned, leading institutes and universities in Japan and the USA through 1985–87, as presented in the book. In the future, such technology will be used in various machines possessing the property of informational consciousness, IC. The IC concept and its possible implementation were newly published under the title "*Informational Recursiveness against Singularity*.[1]

Over the past thirty to forty years, the field of information technology has made tremendous leaps in the size of elementary integration of micro- and nano-components, in operating speed, and in the complex system structure and organization of computer and information systems.

Iskra Delta not only solved advanced technological problems throughout its development, it also developed its own philosophy of progressing into the unknown and upcoming. The employees were aware—at least in terms of the technology—of the historicity of their mission and the extraordinary

---

[1] A. P. Železnikar. 2011. *Informational Recursiveness against Singularity*. Elektrotehniški vestnik. English Edition. 78:3:85–90. Available on http://www.artifico.org or search "Anton Zeleznikar."

organizational efforts made in the complex space of their environment. Iskra Delta meant a new era in the world of the possible, the related, the ingenious, the managerial, and the global. It sat on the opposite bank of traditional provincialism, casualness, and acquiescing to the perceived impossible. It was a school of the new generation, of the creators of new efforts, and achievements of the new generation of businessmen, engineers, and researchers.

Those of us who were blessed with the experience of this new human and entrepreneurial success did not remain idle even after the collapse of Iskra Delta. We were constantly working in this entrepreneurial space, facing the truths that very valuable experience based on combined capacities had been destroyed and that we had to start organizing completely new fundamental business ventures and communities all over again that would not easily achieve the development, production, and business efficiency of the previously combined entrepreneurship. Some ideas have remained, though, and have been cultivated and put into practice. These remain of interest in the global arena of computer and information technology achievements.

Professor Dr. Anton P. Železnikar

# Table of Contents

# Foreword

I have decided to describe the developments in the eighties in the field of information technology which had a significant impact on global change at that time and how the Yugoslavs with our Iskra Delta played a major part, without being sufficiently aware of it all. This was during the height of the Cold War for world supremacy, when the management of information technology brought the most significant advantage on which the United States built its long-term military and economic strategies, while the Soviet Union overlooked that advantage. This was also the time when the U.S. firmly controlled and prevented high-tech exports to other countries, especially to the USSR and China.

I will reveal a very important aspect of the events in the development of information technology in the world and the importance and the unique accidental position that resulted in the founding of the Yugoslav firm Iskra Delta, and its role in the development of and the battle for information technology in the Cold War. This was the tensest period and the turning point of the Cold War, involving the whole world—not only the main protagonists, the United States and the Soviet Union.

Iskra Delta was formed in an environment and time which was unfavourable for entrepreneurial thinking and action, both of which are essential prerequisites for success in the rapidly growing field of information technologies. Due to successful entrepreneurial activity, ambition, courage, and innovation on the part of the employees in the former agency of the American company DEC, within the Elektrotehna company, it was possible to establish a new business that we, the colleagues, named Delta. With its products, business performance, and rapid development, Delta soon began to receive more and more attention, first in Slovenia and then throughout former Yugoslavia.

By joining with Iskra, *Iskra Delta* was formed, which combined the potential of the specialists in the computer field in Slovenia with high-calibre experts from Bosnia and Herzegovina, Montenegro, Croatia, Macedonia, and Serbia. Other companies trying to play a central role in computing in former Yugoslavia paid little attention to the company; other global firms even less. But everything changed when the company obtained and then delivered on the project of China's first computer network for its police agency.

I will also explain some of the events in the ten years of Delta's existence, which until now I did not have the opportunity to speak of, and about which even my colleagues from Iskra Delta know little. I will describe collaboration on projects that attracted the fatal attention of the largest countries, such as the United States, Soviet Union, China, and India, in the eighties, but of which we were not aware at the time due to our enthusiasm for our work.

These countries soon started to monitor Iskra Delta via their intelligence services in Yugoslavia, which was at that time in a privileged position with regard to its access to the latest U.S. information technology. These services found information on developments in the field of information technology in Yugoslavia and the West simply through their representatives, mainly at specialized fairs, such as the electronics fair in Ljubljana and the information technology fair in Zagreb.

Soon Iskra Delta also began presenting its latest information technology-related products at these fairs, including those from their own development as well as those made within the U.S. company DEC, the world's leader in the field of minicomputers at the time. Information technology was evolving rapidly then, but Iskra Delta began to pursue this development with its own solutions in some areas and even anticipate it in certain segments.

It is now indisputable that the U.S. not only prevailed in the Cold War, but also in establishing its superior position in the world; then, to control the world, information technology became one of the most important means. The U.S. still manages and controls such standards and development today.

The role of Iskra Delta in a silent battle between international intelligence services for information technology management was even more important in the eighties, mainly because it developed spontaneously on the initiative of engineers who were ambitious and audacious enough to believe in their own developments and abilities to sell them on the market. That is why nobody in the U.S. could have imagined that someone in the centralist world, especially in the so-called communist world, could develop similarly to their technology firms in Silicon Valley; that also explains why American law on the sale of strategic technologies outside the United States was designed accordingly.

With this book, I would like to tell my colleagues why they had to leave their jobs virtually overnight, as they knew that Iskra Delta had never in its ten-year lifespan been in financial difficulty. At the time, they controlled a significant part of the market in Yugoslavia and the Soviet Union, had completed an extensive project in China, and had tremendous opportunities in India. Iskra Delta already had noticeable success in Western countries and implemented its own development and manufacturing centre in Austria. With its sudden and incomprehensible liquidation at the beginning of 1990, Iskra Delta had invaluable knowledge of technology for those times, competitive products, and huge wealth in its employees as well as its fixed assets. Notwithstanding, the company was declared bankrupt under expedited procedure, which until then had not happened to any company of its size in Yugoslavia.

From the accounts submitted at the beginning of 1989 for the year 1988 by the relevant national authorities, it appears that Iskra Delta's fiscal year 1988 ended with 81 million U.S. dollars in revenue, 8.3 million U.S. dollars in profits, and had more than 2000 employees, over half of whom possessed high if not the highest level of professional education. The company financially supported over 300 students at the faculties in different areas and levels of study and strived to encourage their own staff to further development. Property from the premises and equipment was estimated at 38.5 million U.S. dollars. The company had its own development service units in all the capitals of the Yugoslav republics, which provided support to thousands of users of its computers, and in Nova Gorica, it had one of the most modern school centres in Europe, especially important because it offered, mainly through its experts, complete and continuous education to staff and users of Iskra Delta's solutions in the field of information technology.

There was no comparable company with these results and level of staffing at that time in former Yugoslavia or in all of Europe. Upon its tenth anniversary, in May 1988, people defined it as an example to other companies, as is evident from newspaper comments and statements of former senior government officials. The reader will get an answer to a question that was posed in 1990 and later by many, both the benevolent public and the former Iskra Delta employees: how is it possible and why in a record time of six months, should the company declare bankruptcy, the company which was by the beginning of 1990 one of the most successful Yugoslav and European companies of that time?

I am likely revealing a part of the background action which led to the organized destruction of Iskra Delta, in which former Yugoslav policy officials participated, without, of this I am sure, being fully aware of what they were doing, because they were reliably focused only on their own narrow interests. If they could have estimated how much Iskra Delta's knowledge and its technological solutions were worth at the time, they would have certainly guarded the company as the apple of their eye.

My intention with this book is not to blame anyone for past actions but rather to communicate to readers the importance of the battle for information technology in the Cold War and what role Iskra Delta played in relation to its development and production achievements.

I am sure that the story will be interesting and informative to other readers around the world as well, since information technology had its most dominant development during the Cold War, without which life on this planet would be completely different today.

Finally, I would like to thank all my colleagues in Iskra Delta for their honest and productive cooperation, especially to Dr. Jaro Berce, Tomaž Biber, Marjan Bračko, Jože Buh, Tomislav Djordjević, Rado Faleskini, Tomaž Herman, Janez Kožuh, Danijel Malenšek, Viktor Mrak, Boris Nemec, Božo Oman, Aleš Peršin, Slavko Rožič, and Damjan Žemva, for useful information and suggestions while writing this book.

I owe special thanks to my teacher and professor, Dr. Anton P. Železnikar who stood by me through the writing of my book and encouraged me with his advice and contributions.

Also, very special thanks go to the members of my immediate family; without them this book would probably not exist.

# Chapter 1

# Information Technology (IT) in the World and its Main Institutions and Players from 1970 to 1990

From 1970 to 1990, the big computers from IBM dominated the markets, and an average computer configuration cost more than a million dollars. With their computers, IBM effectively had a global monopoly, as other significant producers like UNIVAC, Borroughs, NCR, Control Data Corporation, General Electric, RCA, and Honeywell together accounted for less than 50 percent of the global market.

The computers of that period were huge; they needed a lot of space and a lot of energy for operating and cooling.

Gene Amdahl tried to undermine this monopoly with the help of the Japanese company Fujitsu, which in 1970 gave money to start the business AMDAHL Corporation, which then developed and sold cheaper IBM-compatible computers (clones of IBM computers).

Fujitsu updated its FACOM with technology it bought from Amdahl, and was able to successfully compete with IBM for some time, primarily in Asia. Gene Amdahl, specifically at a time when he worked for IBM, was recognized as the architect of IBM's most successful 360 series computers, yet Amdahl and Fujitsu failed to seriously undermine IBM in the field of big computers, which were based on centralizing and controlling information processing. Therefore both companies soon ceased production of IBM-compatible computers.

Gene Amdahl set up three more companies in order to compete with IBM, but all these attempts failed as well.

Digital Equipment Corporation (DEC) emerged at the end of 1950s. It was founded in 1957 by Ken Olsen, who had previously worked as an engineer at the Massachusetts Institute of Technology (MIT) Lincoln Laboratory in the development the TX2 computer, already designed on transistor technology. DEC's PDP 1(Programmed Data Processor) meant a new chapter in the philosophy of computer design in the world in 1959. DEC minicomputers were the most widespread, and in use at universities and research institutes in the U.S. and later also in countries in alliance with the United States. PDP 8, PDP 11, and PDP 10 series were mostly used because they provided a wide range of applications, and it was already possible to buy them for less than one hundred thousand dollars.

The major advantage of these computers was that they no longer required so much energy and cooling to operate and were very suitable for the management of various processes and for interactive work.

DEC computers, in addition to classical processing, could process analogue signals in real-time, which, through an analogue digital converter, would become an understandable format for a computer. With these computers, it was possible to work interactively with various terminals, so they were used in computer networks and as workstations.

Because of their universal use and modern design, the American army opted for them for wider use in operational military purposes and to build a network, ARPANET (Advanced Research Project Agency Network), which was commissioned and financed by the U.S. government Department of Defense.

The most important and most widely used computer to manage large computer processes in real time during the eighties was DEC's 32-bit computer Vax (Virtual Address Extension), used in very important strategic systems of the U.S. Army, among other places.

In addition to the leading DEC computers, there were also important minicomputers like HP (Hewlett-Packard) and Data General. HP was founded in 1939 by friends and classmates at the University of Stanford, Bill Hewlett and Dave Packard. Their first product, made in a garage, was an audio oscillator for generating sound effects for Walt Disney Studios. They later moved on to testing and measuring instruments for the audio field.

In the beginning, HP used DEC computers in their electronic measurement systems, but in 1966 it was decided to develop and produce their own minicomputers, which were presented to the market as the HP 2100. Success in this area encouraged the development and manufacture of the first personal computers, the HP 9100, in 1968. These came on the market officially labelled as calculators in order to not immediately and directly compete with IBM.

In 1972, HP also introduced the world's first handheld scientific calculator, the HP 35, which was a leader in this field for a decade.

In the following years, the company progressed rapidly in the development and manufacture of high-tech products through the acquisition of smaller, specialized companies, and became a leading technology company in the areas of personal and laptop computers, servers, software, services for various applications, printers, digital cameras, medical electronic equipment, and other technologically demanding products.

Data General was founded in 1968 by Edson de Castro, who was previously a notable product engineer for the successful series of DEC's 12-bit minicomputers PDP 8. Since DEC's president, Ken Olsen, did not support upgrading the PDP 8 in a 16-bit version, de Castro left DEC to later compete successfully with them through his own company and their minicomputers Nova, Super Nova, and Eclipse, which had the greatest success in universities, institutes, and in air traffic control systems.

The U.S. had an effective monopoly in the field of mini-computers, as well, with these companies covering more than 80 percent of the global market.

An important milestone in development took place in 1971 when Ted Hoff at Intel invented and produced a microprocessor with his colleagues: a single chip containing most of the logical components of a computer. With this, he established Intel, which was founded by Gordon Moore and Robert Noyce, and became the leading supplier of microprocessors for the new field of microcomputers in the world.

Only a few inches in size, the microprocessor chip was made on a base plate of silicon and had equal ability and power as the ENIAC, the 18,000 electronic vacuum tubes, several tons heavier and tens of cubic meters larger computer, which was one of the first computers made, twenty years earlier.

Since then, the so-called Moore's Law has entered into force, which states that the number of transistors that can be installed on a specified surface of silicon doubles every two and a half years.

In early 1975, the Altair 8800 appeared in the U.S. as the first 8-bit microcomputer; then came hundreds of others, among which the most important were from Apple, Commodore, and Radio Shack, which produced machines running with CP/M operating systems. Featuring 8-bit processors, they managed a small but rapidly growing market of computers at the time. Data flow through these small computers was running as on an eight-lane highway, contrary to the mini and large computers where it ran on thirty-two or more lanes. Eight "lanes" was not insignificant considering that Apple and others were trying to reach a large computer platform and they all wanted to put their own computer on the table for about three thousand dollars.

Most new ideas came from the Xerox Research Centre PARC in Palo Alto in that period, but Xerox itself could not realize them in time for the market. With the emergence of 16-bit microprocessors in 1981 and 1982, manufacturers

were no longer looking for role models in large computers, but looked for those new roles and ideas in themselves.
Most new ideas were still coming from PARC, as the computer technology used until the end of the last century was
invented there.

Even IBM began to realize in the early eighties that it would
not be able to survive without a microcomputer, so it put the
first personal computer on the market at the end of 1981,
manufactured by a renegade unit in Florida. IBM decided
to produce and market its first microcomputer as a separate
unit so as not to interfere with the rest of IBM's new business,
which was then one of the largest companies in the world.
In this unit, therefore, the IBM-PC was only designed, but it
was created from parts of other already-established manufacturers of computer components; here Microsoft played
a special role, with its founder, Bill Gates, who managed to
persuade the project manager of the IBM-PC to make the
16-bit version of the Intel processor.

For this processor, IBM needed operating software, which
Bill Gates did not have, so he bought it from the company
Seattle Computer Products and then sold it to IBM, which
needed it badly but could not buy it from Digital Research,
which was, as a result of special circumstances, the leading
manufacturer of operating software. This move allowed Bill
Gates to develop Microsoft and standardize writing application programs for Microsoft's MS-DOS, and not for CP/M
from Digital Research. Although Digital Research had the
most advanced product then, it did not command the market laws.

Bill Gates probably would not have experienced such success without his father's strategic and timely legal advice; he
was one of the best and most influential lawyers in the U.S.
at that time. His mother also had an important role in his
contacts with IBM because she was a good acquaintance of
the then-president of IBM, with whom she made friends
while participating in committees for charitable activities. As
a student with such support, Bill Gates could already reach

influential people at IBM and also get the best legal advice on concrete contracts, without which he would certainly not have had such success in his dealings with IBM; as a result the mighty IBM became dependent on him and not vice versa.

Gary Kildall, the founder of Digital Research, was rapidly satisfied with his then-monopolistic position in the operating system market with his CP/M for Intel processors. He earned a lot of money quickly and easily, but he did not use it for business expansion, instead focusing more on personal entertainment, cars and airplanes. He took advantage of the fact that he himself had made, following Intel's order, the first CP/M operating software for Intel processors, and for the DEC multi-user PDP 10 computer, which was a very important development tool in U.S. universities in the seventies. Of those countries not in the NATO alliance, with the exception of Switzerland, the only country to own this computer in 1980 was Yugoslavia, at the University of Ljubljana, on the basis of special permission from the American administration.

On such a DEC computer, Bill Gates and Bob Allen also developed their own programming language: Basic.

The operating system (the software) is the soul of every computer. It is important for the functioning of the computer, as the user speaks to the operating system and the operating system then speaks to the processor. Among many other tasks, the operating system controls and manages the flow of data between the processor and its permanent memory. Operating systems typically store data on a disk in files that have their names and properties, and the program calls them when they are needed by the user.

At that time, it was very important in the development of microcomputers that IBM invented the eight-inch floppy disk, which was intended to replace punch cards in their computers and was precisely what Kildall needed in the development of CP/M for external memory. Because of his pride, Kildall did not want to integrate Microsoft's Basic programming language in his operating system at the time, which largely resulted in him losing the leading role on the market and further enabled Microsoft to take over. Still, IBM decisively contributed to

Microsoft's victory in the operating system market; they rapidly conquered the emerging market of microcomputers with large quantities and attractive pricing, so that most other producers could not withstand the pace, even though IBM did not produce its own computer and its technology was not the most advanced in relation to the competition at the time. IBM had its product made by its co-operators, but marketed it all under the IBM brand name through its unique distribution network, which was then the largest in the world.

The leaders of IBM were unaware then that their PC did not have much IBM in it. Theirs was only the BIOS, which connected the IBM hardware to the Microsoft operating system. Microsoft, based on a good contract with IBM, retained the right to sell MS-DOS to other companies, as IBM had relied only on the earnings that they intended to achieve through quantities and let other companies manufacture compatible computers and write application programs for MS-DOS, out of which only Microsoft had much to gain. Once IBM recognized this, it was already too late for action.

At that time, in addition to the previously mentioned companies, other important players had entered the computer field:

> COMPAQ was the first to clone the IBM computers on a large scale and advanced to overcome IBM's development with time.
>
> CRAY RESEARCH, founded by Seymour Cray, built the first supercomputer, the CRAY I, in 1976 on vector-based architecture; it then achieved a speed of more than 10 megaflops (ten million floating point operations per second) and was the fastest computer in the world.
>
> NOVELL, in 1983, dominated the integration of PCs in the network at least as well as IBM had linked the market of personal computers.
>
> LOTUS 1-2-3, with their spreadsheets, had the most popular user program, and worked on most computers.

3COM, with its founder and main innovator Bob Metcalfe, the inventor of Ethernet networking software, enabled connection of the most popular computers on the market at the time.

ORACLE was the first name of the project prototype for the manufacture of relational database software commissioned by the U.S. Central Intelligence Agency (CIA). The CIA got the basis for the project from the publication of IBM's development, in which Dr. Edgar F. Codd was the first to explain and describe the concept of a relational database. Larry Ellison and Bob Miner, who worked on this project, sensed a great opportunity for commercial exploitation on the market. To this end, they founded a company in 1979, Relational Software Incorporation (RSI), and then because of the success they had with their second published version of the software, renamed the company the ORACLE Corporation in 1983, which then, through innovation and aggressive performance on the market, became a leading company in the world in a rapidly developing field.

The U.S. Defense Advanced Research Projects Agency (DARPA), due to the requirement to develop high-performance workstations, allowed the foundation of SUN Microsystems. This company was formed by experts from Stanford University, and subsequently developed into a leading manufacturer of technological workstations based on UNIX. It used Ethernet for connections. SUN was the first to find out that the easiest way to establish a de facto standard was to give away the source code for free. This bestowal of the source code allowed SUN to set the standard; they were then the first to manufacture hardware based on it, which corresponded to that standard.

As SUN needed a more powerful processor for their workstation but could not acquire one on the market, they designed their own and named it SPARC. Due to its design, purchasing components for manufacturing its processor was cheaper for SUN than for other computer manufacturers; thus it started to dominate the workstation market, also penetrating other markets, which were previously dominated by IBM and DEC. SUN gave their system software for free, so to speak, and in doing so, they basically encouraged the cloning of their own hardware. This meant that, to maintain their leading market position, they would be forced to develop new, more powerful SPARC computers at a faster rate. This would be managed by their competitors, notably DEC and IBM, which tried unsuccessfully to confront them, namely the DEC with the RISC processor by the MIPS Computer Systems and IBM with its own RISC processor. HP preferred to arrange with SUN to develop programs jointly and did not waste as much money as IBM and DEC. It is interesting that the RISC processor was envisioned at IBM, an acronym for "reduced instruction set computing".

These were the most typical battles, and most of them were happening only apparently, since the U.S. government had long monitored and even encouraged them, but took great care to make sure that it all happened only within the U.S. The export of this technology was controlled with specific legislation, particularly to countries that were not in its closest alliance. By encouraging competition in development and thus the competitive struggle between businesses in the area of information technologies, they also wanted to shake the mastodon IBM, which relied too heavily on its power and monopoly and was, therefore, much slower in developing technologies than the competitors.

With the rapid development of microcomputers and their capabilities, and with the rapid development of system and user software and computer networks, it became increasingly obvious that the future was not in large and expensive computers, but in personal computers and workstations connected to the network.

Bill Gates and his Microsoft were only too well aware of this.

Increasingly clear, also, was the fact that the development and production of processors, system and network software, and management of standards in this area were to be of strategic importance in the future, not the computers themselves or creating application programs for different fields of use.

As Bill Gates said at the beginning of his career at the establishment of Microsoft, only the management of standards brings big money, so he focused most of his energy on making his products the world standard, which made him the richest man on the planet.

Due to the central, state planned way of managing their economies, the companies in countries that fell within the area of interest of the Soviet Union could not be equally involved in the struggle regarding the field of information technology. They were subject to state planning; even the creation of new businesses was stipulated every five years by the state plan.

This rapidly evolving area of computing got its start-up with the companies in Silicon Valley that were based on self-initiative and innovation, and in which individuals could immediately transfer into practice the ideas they obtained at universities and institutes. They were able to achieve this by rapidly establishing new companies and competitive functioning on the market.

In contrast, the planned economy did not allow this, so the companies set up by countries in the East were increasingly left behind, which was especially evident in the seventies and eighties with the emergence of mini and microcomputers, which increased the development of information technology to such an extent that even companies in Western Europe had difficulty following this rapid development and, therefore, increasingly lagged behind.

What yet further contributed to this was the aggressive performance of the new American companies, which were always ahead of the European ones with their new products and competitive prices, and, therefore, began to exercise their own standards in the U.S. for both the hardware and software fields, all of which caused insurmountable problems for the companies outside the U.S.

Iskra Delta followed this rapid development in Europe mostly during the eighties because, in accordance with the OEM (Original Equipment Manufacturer) and the generic principle, it developed and produced its own computers and solutions that were compatible and comparable with the U.S. computers, and as competitive, especially because, in this field, the U.S. companies had charged Europe more than 50 percent higher prices than at home in the U.S.

Due to the formation of Iskra Delta in a hostile environment that did not allow initiative and where it was mostly subordinate to state regulation and the decisions of the Party, Iskra Delta's development was hindered in Yugoslavia. It had been created and developed in an unusual way for those times. Delta's developments and results were not seriously considered at home, in the beginning, in Slovenia and Yugoslavia, and even less abroad. U.S. companies initially underestimated it, not paying attention until after it joined the Iskra system and only then became aware of its first major international project on its own, which they thought would not be realized without their help. By the time it actually delivered the project, Iskra Delta had already managed a number of key components of development and produced products in the field of information technology.

# Chapter 2

# IBM Strategy in Dealing with the Computer Market in the World

IBM, founded in 1924, has its roots in the Tabulating Machine Company, which was founded in 1860 by Herman Hollerith, who was born near New York. He invented and patented the data storage for business applications on punch cards, which were an early medium for storing programs and data in his machinery and later in the early computers.

IBM switched to the field of development and manufacturing of electronic computers in the early fifties on the basis of U.S. Department of Defense contracts and with the experts who already had experience in making the first computer in Britain during the Second World War, which was primarily designed to destroy German communications codes.

IBM did not build their empire of big computers on computer capacity, mass production, or lower prices, but on reliable service and was, therefore, from the end of 1970 to early 1980, the most profitable company in the world. In the late seventies and early eighties, the company had such power that they set standards for the implementation of computers in the larger companies in the world, thereby enabling the increasing inflow of profits from around the world into the U.S., from companies and countries that wanted to progress and insisted on having their large and expensive computers. During this period, a lot of programs were written for them, especially for business operations and to assist administrations in the management of countries. But more and more companies, especially in the U.S., eventually realized that the work could be not only done with big and expensive computers, but could also be done with mini and even personal computers. This corporate powerhouse, therefore, began work in the field of personal computers, but in a manner that would not adversely affect its business with large computers.

The initial success of IBM in personal computers was almost entirely a web of fortunate coincidences. Due to a conservative and monopolistic way of management, the company, which at that time was not able to invent something new in less than three years, managed to produce a personal computer and associated operating system within one year by giving the rights for it to be produced outside the company. IBM purchased its components from existing small businesses and then put it on the market through its huge distribution network under the name IBM-PC. From 1981 to 1984, IBM also postulated criteria for personal computers, allowing American and other companies to make PCs. The company seriously and literally created the economic sector as we know it today, but lost control of personal computers after 1984. Reality caught up with the department for small systems when the development of PC-AT was completed. Since then, IBM has taken three years or more to develop and market each new family of computers.

Using criteria that apply to large computers, three years was not much. Personal computers, which must follow the curve of the relationship between price and performance, as with semiconductors, had to double the capacity every two and a half years. IBM was no longer able to do this, but its smaller rivals were, and the company that stood out most was Compaq. IBM established Microsoft MS-DOS as the standard operating system. They set the standard for 16-bit guidance on the PC-AT, which determined the form of additional cards from different manufacturers to be used in the same machine. These were the criteria kindly contributed by the leader to the rivals because the company needed assistance from other companies to produce hardware and software to help them conquer more markets. In doing so, IBM lost its leadership on the capacity curve, but its standards were still considered a signpost for the IBM PC clone makers who gradually came to the foreground on the market.

IBM had to helplessly observe their market share decrease due to the wrong decisions of its managers; however, it was still a major player in the business with PCs, still had the most opportunities to confuse the technical world, and knew best how to slow down the development of the computer market, which was done in several ways.

First, IBM effectively confused the competition by announcing the development of a trend, but not the resulting product, thereby causing buyers to wait for the new generation of machines, and then IBM announced that it had changed its mind.

Second, they announced the real product, but much earlier than they were able to put it on the market. This endangered the competitive companies that already sold such products, as potential buyers waited for the acquisition, because with it, they would get a more powerful and less expensive product.

Then IBM did not announce the product again, but made sure that the public got a few strategic tips that were not true and the competition was left, again, waiting for what would happen. All the while, IBM continued to sell the older computers to its buyers, and earned well.

IBM did not support foreign standards, and favoured their own. This was best seen when all other manufacturers connected their computers with Ethernet while IBM invented its own technology: Token Ring. When all others were convinced that the best operating system on workstations was Unix, IBM insisted on its OS/2, which was actually a much weaker system.

IBM counted on its influence to help establish its own standard and spoil the joy of its competitors. The OS/2 operating system, which they entrusted Microsoft to develop and which filled them with the hope that it would stop the further spread of MS-DOS, was a sad failure. Sales were tenuous, and the capacity was incredibly small.

By 1989, Microsoft took into account the IBM leadership, publicly advocated OS/2, and promised versions of all its main applications which would run under this operating system. On the outside, the relationships with IBM appeared good. In fact, after careful consideration, Bill Gates decided that DOS, and not OS/2, was good for Microsoft; he proposed to IBM that it abandon further development of OS/2, which IBM did not accept.

Microsoft started to abandon the development of OS/2 as it became clear that abandonment of DOS would not be of any use. At that critical time, when the further fate of Microsoft was being decided, Bill Gates found a "best solution." He upgraded DOS with Windows. Following his ideas, Windows preserved the strategic value of DOS for Microsoft and gave users most of the features of OS/2, which Gates increasingly used only as an operating system for network servers. IBM wanted to take the baton from the hands of Microsoft, with which it would set the world standard operating system on personal computers by replacing DOS with OS/2. Bill Gates realized this in time and instructed his engineers to slow down the development of OS/2, especially its graphical interface.

After months of negotiations, IBM and Microsoft reached an agreement in 1990 which left DOS and Windows to Microsoft, and OS/2 to IBM. Windows was a tremendous success for Microsoft, selling over three million copies the first year after the presentation. It had, in terms of developing programs, a great advantage at the beginning over those who tried to copy it and who would exploit the advantages of Windows. With this, Microsoft managed to firmly anchor itself as the first IT company for personal computers.

After the success of Windows, IBM sought to find a new image recognizable to all, but was faced with difficulty. It used the same old trick again and announced the latest product, then said it was not serious about the hardware and software for connecting PCs to the network PC-LAN, which could jeopardize sales and profits of its big computers with multiple terminals.

IBM, however, could not endanger the development of network computing with its tricks and monopolies. Because of its insistence on the concept of large computers and rigid organization, it came into serious crisis by the early nineties, as Bill Gates had already announced, and it would also fail without a new president who could establish not only a different strategy, but above all, the right strategy, for the nineties.

The new president took into account in his strategy the fact that IBM had lost the battle in the market of personal computers, and this is why his strategy was, in addition to promoting the development and production of large computers and workstations, mainly based on computer communications services and the impending arrival of the Internet. In doing so, IBM took full advantage, by prevailing with the already installed database on its users' computers around the world. This allowed IBM to offer its users comprehensive business solutions and included help for users in those organizations to achieve better business results on the basis of using its computers and software solutions.

# Chapter 3

# The Role of Tito and Yugoslavia in the Cold War

The Cold War began soon after World War II. The main protagonists were the United States and USSR, each with their own allies which had been liberated from German occupation by these two large powers. Yugoslavia, with Tito as the head of state, was an ally with his partisans to the U.S. as well as to the USSR during the war. In Europe, Yugoslavia was the only country liberated mainly by its own forces, although Soviet soldiers did help to liberate a minor part of the country. By the end of World War II, Tito had an army with around 800,000 members. This was a state-of-the-art army because most of the weapons were acquired by confiscating the Germans'; others were received from the USSR and the USA. It is due to this self-liberation that the country was in a unique position to maintain its allies, both Western and Eastern.

Immediately after the war, Yugoslavia came into serious conflict with the Western allies who forced Yugoslavia and its army to leave liberated Trieste, a multiethnic city in the North-East of today's Italy, with Slovenians as a large minority living in the city.

This led to such strained relations with the Western allies that it almost led to a conflict, since immediately following the war, Yugoslavs shot down or forced the landings of many Western aircraft that attempted to fly over the disputed territories without permission. Tito came into conflict with its ally to the east, USSR, due to the ideological differences and the tendency of the USSR and its leader, Stalin, to treat Yugoslavia in the same way as it treated countries liberated by the Soviet army. Because of this conflict, Yugoslavia was never pulled behind the so-called Iron Curtain, as were the other countries occupied by the Soviet army.

Westerners, with the British and Americans as leaders, gradually began to view Tito's dispute with Stalin sympathetically, since Tito and his army represented an important force in case a confrontation arose between them in the Cold War. This is why the West started to help Yugoslavia in the conflict with Stalin and the USSR, initially with equipment for industry and food and later with armament.

Regardless of this, Yugoslavia, with its leader Marshal Tito, faced considerable solitude for some time in 1948, until Tito gave the initiative for a meeting with Nasser, President of Egypt, Nehru, President of India, Sukarno, President of Indonesia, and Nkrumah, President of Ghana, who established the Non-Aligned Movement. It was founded in Belgrade in 1961 and Tito became the first president of the movement. In the sixties, at the height of its power, the Movement demanded and succeeded in persuading the United Nations that in all laws, international agreements, and memoranda on the oceans, space, and Antarctica, all of which were adopted then, that among other things, those which would develop and manage to develop high technology for their exploration and use would also have to share it with the least developed countries.

This made it possible for Tito to gradually improve relations with the West, notably Britain. In London as early as 1950, he met with British Prime Minister Churchill, the British Queen, and with leaders in the United States of America, who soon began gradually helping Yugoslavia economically and militarily.

After Stalin's death, the USSR policy toward Yugoslavia became warmer, as Stalin's successor, Khrushchev, acknowledged the mistake that Stalin had made politically with regard to Yugoslavia. After Khrushchev visited Yugoslavia, relations with the USSR improved significantly, so that Tito, with his Yugoslavia, represented a real bridge between the superpowers during the tensest period of the Cold War.

In 1963, Tito was on an official visit to the U.S. to meet President Kennedy, where the U.S. President confirmed the independence of Yugoslavia and its leadership in the growing number of countries in the Non-Aligned Movement, and confirmed that this policy of Tito's had beneficial effects on the tension prevailing in the Cold War between the East and West. Kennedy particularly stressed the important contribution of Tito and his army to the victory in the Second World War, and his role after the war in establishing new relations between different countries, which had earlier been recognized by Kennedy's predecessors, Presidents Eisenhower and Truman.

The influence and reputation of Yugoslavia and the role of the Non-Aligned Movement was such that at the end of July 1965, U.S. President Lyndon Johnson sent his ambassador to meet with Tito on the islands of Brijuni for consultations regarding the U.S. withdrawal from Vietnam. In return for Tito's constructive cooperation in resolving the Vietnamese crisis, the U.S. government supported Yugoslav economic reforms and in 1965 Yugoslavia began allowing foreign business investments, the first socialist country to do so.

Tito's active policy of peace and the struggle for neutrality of Yugoslavia in relation to the major players of the Cold War, the U.S. and USSR, and the strengthening of the role of the Non-Aligned Movement in the world in the most tense years of the Cold War enhanced the reputation of Yugoslavia and Tito in such a manner that Richard Nixon, the first president of the U.S. to do so, visited Yugoslavia at the beginning of October 1970. This showed immense recognition of Tito's role in the world, he who greatly contributed to the balance of forces in Europe and the world with his Non-Aligned Movement policy.

In 1971, Tito visited the U.S. for the second time, and this visit with U.S. President Nixon was particularly successful because, at that time, Yugoslavia acquired the status in trade and cooperation with the U.S. that only NATO members and neutral countries such as Switzerland and Austria were granted. This visit also contributed to the fact that the Yugo-slav people could then obtain U.S. visas much more easily, which made education in America possible, and made establishing business relations with the American companies simpler. These good relations with the United States were even more evident in August 1975, when President Gerald Ford visited Yugoslavia, where, among other things, he signed an agreement on credit and a purchase agreement for the construction of an American nuclear plant with 600 MW power in Yugoslavia. This was in order to improve relations that had cooled due to conflicting views on the Arab-Israeli conflict in 1973.

The fact that Tito refused the request of the visit of Soviet President Brezhnev to Yugoslavia in 1976, the purpose of which was to allow Soviet naval bases in the Adriatic Sea and the freedom of passage to Soviet aircraft flying over the Yugoslavian territory, was also very important for good relations with the U.S.

President Tito last visited the U.S. in 1978, when he and the Yugoslav delegation had successful talks with U.S. President Carter and his staff in Washington. This visit helped to further improve the technological and military cooperation and the particularly special status that Yugoslavia had when it came to favourable trade with the U.S. Good relations with the West, especially with the U.S., allowed Yugoslavia to open to the world even more. A growing number of Yugoslav people began working abroad and tourism began to develop very quickly, as well, having a strong influence on the rapid economic development at that time.

Highly influential American Jews also helped the good relations between the United States and Yugoslavia, since Yugoslavia had played an important role in the establishment and recognition of the country of Israel in the United Nations and with having enabled Jews to escape from concentration camps to Palestine during World War II and right after it, then in the face of the strong opposition especially by the British.

Very important for the neutral and non-aligned status of Yugoslavia were President Tito's visit to Beijing in 1977 and President Hua Guofeng's visit to Belgrade, which improved relations between the two countries and increased economic cooperation between them. The countries were in ideological conflict prior to these visits in much the same way as with the Soviet Union.

The company's origins and its role in the battle for information technology in the Cold War is later discussed in this book.

# Chapter 4

# How Delta Formed

Iskra Delta had its roots of development in human resources, which were derived from the newly established Department of Computer Science at the Faculty of Electrical Engineering, University of Ljubljana, and from the Department for Representation of Foreign Companies in the Slovenian commercial company Elektrotehna from Ljubljana.

The International Federation for Information Processing (IFIP) congress, held in 1971 in Ljubljana thanks to two leading professors of informatics at the University of Ljubljana, had a significant impact on the development of informatics in Yugoslavia and especially in Slovenia. The development of informatics in Slovenia has its roots in the Department of Digital Engineering at the Jožef Stefan Institute and the University of Ljubljana. On this basis, there were already people with the right knowledge, people who had graduated from this department at that time with the ability to organize the development of their computers. These people were also highly sought after by foreign, mainly U.S., companies that represented and sold computers in Slovenia.

In early 1970, the big, state-owned Elektrotehna firm specialized in selling electro-technical products to companies in Yugoslavia and was, among other things, authorized to import and export these products. In early 1972, regarding the import of complex automated systems for the needs of state institutions, they came into contact with the American computer company Digital Equipment Corporation (DEC), which was something new on the market at that time with its minicomputers, and was the leader in its field, as well as serious competition to IBM, the main producer of computers.

IBM already had an established agent in Yugoslavia at that time, the Intertrade company in Ljubljana, which sold with a huge profit their big computers, mainly to banks and large state companies. The leaders in Elektrotehna opted to represent the prestigious American computer company DEC and sell its computers, so they signed an exclusive contract for sales in Yugoslavia and, under its direction, established a specialized department for representation. This contract contained a provision that it would take effect only when the first Elektrotehna engineer, chosen for this work, had successfully completed special training in DEC in the U.S. Based on this provision, Elektrotehna sent the very engineer who suggested this cooperation for training in America and, after successful completion of the prescribed school, he became the first Director of the Special Department, specializing in the sale and servicing of DEC computers in Yugoslavia.

This newly created department had great success in sales after a few months and soon brought increasing earnings to Elektrotehna, obtained by commission for sold computers and maintenance services. On this basis, it became more and more important from year to year that the leaders were able to obtain an increasing number of new professionals and send them for education abroad; this is the reason they could expand their sales in all the former republics of Yugoslavia in such a short time. The Special Department, which was soon renamed to Digital, was mainly composed of able and ambitious engineers. They eventually were no longer satisfied with only selling and servicing computers, so they extended their activities to the field of applied software.

Gradually, the Digital department, which began its development and production operations in the basement of a renovated boiler room in Ljubljana, started to offer more complete custom solutions and services of their own to users on the Yugoslav market. They initially purchased computers to manage processes in industry and research institutes, and then, more and more, turned to manage business processes. With such an entrepreneurial orientation in the department, they increased their earnings and their importance in Elektrotehna.

Due to aggressive marketing of their services, they became ever more visible and competitive in the markets of Yugo-slavia, since the solutions of their engineers had the same quality but at a lower price than the customers were pay-ing engineers of foreign companies in Yugoslavia for similar work, and in particular for software solutions and services. Such a market orientation enabled more than 300 percent annual growth in both business volume and the number of employees for the Digital department. Due to similar success on the market, at the end of 1977, the Digital department had grown into an independent, specialized computer company called Delta, but remained within the Elektrotehna company, which was then transformed into a joint venture.

At that time, it was important to acquire foreign currency for imports of computers. Foreign currency was something only companies with exports to countries that paid in con-vertible currencies had. These were mainly wood industry companies, so Delta began to link with them, especially with those which already had or intended to buy DEC computers for their needs.

This was a time of great shortage of foreign currency assets in the entire former Yugoslavia. Imports of reproductive mate-rial had an advantage over imports of equipment, the group to which computers belonged. These imports were not subject to a special committee in Belgrade, which allowed the use of for-eign exchange for imports of equipment. The then-Yugoslav government policy stipulated that export companies that exceeded their export plans could use a part of their foreign currencies for their own use or sell them at a special price to other companies for the import of reproductive material. This option to purchase foreign currencies in the so-called foreign exchange market was taken advantage of especially by those important manufacturing companies which were not mainly export-oriented to the Western markets.

Due to serious difficulties with the acquisition of licenses for imports of computers, Delta undertook the project of producing their own computer, a computer compatible to DEC according to the OEM (Original Equipment Manufacturer) principles, just as similar companies in the U.S. already did. Their first computer was designed in such a manner that it only had critical components from the DEC presentational program. For all simple components, such as power supply, cooling, and computer chassis, they used domestic ones already being produced to high quality standards in Slovenia. A significant self-contribution of Delta was in the Delta-developed applicative computer software, which made it far easier to obtain the status of a domestic product.

This trend of Delta in the production of their own computer was essential to their further development, since in this way they managed to import those components of a computer that could not be purchased in Yugoslavia as reproductive material and not as equipment, which was subject to obtaining permits from a special commission. Quotas for imports of equipment were shared centrally for the whole country in Belgrade, and this was why the import of computers was not possible without the approval of a special commission in Belgrade, which caused major problems mainly to companies which, in this way, were not able to modernize the same way as competitive companies in the West. Due to the growing demands of the Yugoslav economy to import computers, for which significant foreign currencies funds were diverted, the government of that time decided that the state-owned companies in the field of electronics, which were distributed across the republics, must organize in a way to jointly begin production of computers made in Yugoslavia and in this way satisfy the requirements of the army and also reduce the use of foreign currency funds. These companies were in other republics, and among them competition already ruled. They were signing contracts independently of each other with U.S. companies for the licensed production of computers.

These computers, which were offered by the U.S. companies for licensed production, were no longer competitive on the U.S. market due to rapid development. In addition to the sale of licensing, these companies also sensed additional income in the increased sales of the components of their computers, since they could be easily exported to Yugoslavia because their computers were assembled in Yugoslavia and thus had the status of a domestic product. American companies could export their computer equipment to Yugoslavia because Yugoslavia had non-aligned status at the time and had a particularly favourable position with the American government based on an agreement between Yugoslav President Tito and U.S. President Carter on the export of technological products from the U.S. in relation to other countries from the East and from the undeveloped world.

The U.S. government classified every country in the world into different categories according to their strategic importance to the United States at the time of the Cold War. The U.S. technology companies obtained export licenses for Yugoslavia more easily, which contractually guaranteed that it would not allow the export of these technologies, particularly computers, without special permission from the U.S. government, into the third world countries.

Regardless of this, Delta was in a difficult position. Especially because it was founded in a commercial company, it could not be classified in the electronics industry according to the law while having its own development and production capacities. Entrepreneurial activity was also not desirable; therefore, it was unwise for the company to consider manufacturing computers independently because then the government would decide on everything according to the approved state plans; self-initiative was the most complicating factor most of the time.

The solution was to convince the republic's government first, and then the federal government, that Delta had the necessary knowledge to be able to obtain the required initial production capacities without major investments, and that it was able to manufacture computers under its own plan without purchasing a license, which was contrary to the Yugoslav law at the time.

# Chapter 5

# Delta 340: Production and Presentation of the First Computer

Delta engineers realized, on the basis of successful cooperation with DEC, that they could take advantage of the fact that DEC had sales to buyers who had computers built into their original products and devices according to the OEM rule. Based on this insight and knowledge, acquired during those five years working on independent installations and servicing DEC computers, they decided to make a computer model of their own design and configuration. It was designed so that Delta bought only the processor PDP and the operating software from the DEC company. The remaining units of the computer were bought from other original manufacturers in the world that were also occasional suppliers for DEC. Their own applicative software was then added to such a computer, plus the domestic electronic solutions that enabled computer operation in a configuration that was not prescribed by DEC and was not composed only of DEC components, but nevertheless was computer compatibility with DEC computers, which were still being imported at the time by Elektrotehna for their customers in Yugoslavia.

Since Elektrotehna had difficulties obtaining import licenses for importing computers to Belgrade, and due to the sizable earnings of Elektrotehna through Delta, the management decided to close down one of the stores and to allow Delta to rearrange the space in the computing centre. It was there that the Delta engineers, in record time, developed and did what was necessary to be able to build their first computer, with only the bare minimum of DEC components.

In doing so, they encountered a big problem importing the needed DEC components and the components of other suppliers from abroad. The problem was specific in that Elektrotehna was not a manufacturing company and had no license from the state for the import of components, assemblies, and sub-assemblies as reproductive material. The problem was resolved so that the parts and sub-assemblies needed from foreign suppliers for the first computer were imported as spare parts rather than as equipment. With this decision, they gained a great deal of time, since the bureaucratic procedures for obtaining appropriate authorization were avoided. Since the parts for this computer were bought from the original producers, they were also more than 100 percent cheaper than those offered by DEC. This product, which included a lot of knowledge and work, was cheaper and thus more acceptable to customers, and still allowed considerable earnings for Delta. In addition to better opportunities in the market, the additional argument for the enthusiasm in the work of building their own computer was the knowledge that this would benefit the country as a whole, since it would use its own products and use less foreign currency than was then required for the import of computers.

To obtain the status of producer, they had to first convince the professional public and the state bureaucracy that the computer they were about to present was really made mostly at home and not imported. They were aware that mainly domestic importers and agents of competing computers would try to prevent them from gaining better conditions for import licenses through the status of being a manufacturer of the domestic computer. In addition to the professional public, it was difficult to convince the politicians, as most of the initiatives that were not agreed upon in advance with them were doomed to fail, and in some cases, were even criminally punishable.

To avoid this, Delta had to get on the good side of both of these factors, without which this kind of behaviour would be considered arbitrary, and would be harmful and even criminal for the management of Delta and, in particular, Elektrotehna.

To be as convincing as possible, they decided to name the computer *Delta*. Because the letter delta is the fourth letter of the Greek alphabet, the name represented the fourth and latest computer generation. At the same time, the name was also a link with the company name. This was the first Yugoslav computer made at home and for which there was no need to pay licensing charges.

The most important thing for the entire project was the computer presentation to the Yugoslav public, because this was not a pre-agreed product, but the result of self-initiative, created in the way that similar companies worked in Silicon Valley at the time. Also, it was not made in a company that was among the existing electronics companies, but in a wrong place, in a commerce organization which was not registered for development and production.

Delta nevertheless managed to choose the right way to attract the Yugoslav public, especially the journalists and politicians who attended the presentation. The solution was found in the birthday celebration of Marshal Tito, the president of the country, who was the only undisputed authority in the former Yugoslavia.

On May 25, for his birthday, Tito annually received congratulations from all over Yugoslavia, particularly from the young. The engineers in Elektrotehna were still mostly young people. They took advantage of that and decided to publicly present him with the first computer made in Yugoslavia for his birthday. This move was intended to solve the problem of their presence at the event and give the presentation pan-Yugoslav exposure. To do this, it was necessary to do something special, something truly theirs, so that the whole thing would not sound like a provocation. They decided to make a music model and program for the Yugoslav national anthem, and a model and computer program for Tito's portrait to be drawn by the computer at the opening ceremony.

This is something that had never been done in Yugoslavia before. The general public was largely not aware that a computer could play music and draw a picture.

They had very little time for the implementation of these ideas, so all the employees at Delta had to make great efforts to develop and complete everything on time, in the few months that were available. And there was a lot to do, as in addition to the transfer of development work into recognizable products, it was also necessary to carry out all the organizational, spatial, and staff additions. As Delta did not have adequate facilities for the presentation, it was necessary to gain the support of the management and political organizations of Elektrotehna in a short time to make all this possible.

This support was substantial, given that the managements of Delta and Elektrotehna were aware of what it was they were about to do together and that they had very little time for the realization. Due to the adopted resolution at the Elektrotehna national labour committee on the abolition of commercial premises, which were the most suitable for conversion into a place to produce a computer as well as for the presentation to the public, there was an unexpected complication. A tragic part was the fact that the shop manager, who emotionally could not stand its suspension, committed suicide during the refurbishment of the shop into the computation centre. This endangered the entire presentation project, as opponents of the computer presentation in Elektrotehna began to openly interfere with the work of preparing the centre, one of the most critical points of the project.

With the great enthusiasm of all the employees at Delta and the leaders at Elektrotehna, they managed to accomplish all the work required for a successful computer presentation to the public just one day before the opening. The opening and presentation at Tito's birthday celebration on May 25, 1978, saw complete success because, fortunately, everything worked as expected. It was attended by the rector of the University of Ljubljana, and even some city and republic officials, headed by the Vice President of the National government.

In the invitation to selected journalists, politicians, and businessmen, it was stated that the performance and display of the domestic computer would take place on the day of Tito's birthday, in his honour.

In particular, all who were invited were interested to know what the first unlicensed computer made in Yugoslavia, one that could play the Yugoslav national anthem and draw a portrait of Tito, looked like. Journalists attended in large numbers, since this presentation was a complete shock for them, as well. They were from the editorial boards of most of the republics and wrote extensively of the achievement, dedicated, without saying, of course, to Tito for his birthday. This idea was also a shock for the Yugoslav politicians, none of whom dared to prevent the presentation or the release of the achievement, especially when it was dedicated to Tito. Some prominent bureaucrats, on the other hand, tried everything to prevent the release, mainly because such an initiative was not desirable and in line with the national plan. Others were against the production of such products from the so-called electro-industry of Yugoslavia.

But, for Delta, it was particularly important that journalists wrote according to the presentation that was heard at the opening, that the computer really was made in Yugoslavia and not in the U.S.; otherwise it would not be possible to present it to Tito. At the opening, the representatives of the young read the congratulations sent in the form of telegram to Brijuni, where Tito was then living. Proof that the presentation was a complete surprise is the fact that he did not immediately receive the birthday telegram, since there were personnel in his cabinet who tried to stop something that was not previously agreed upon. However, because well-intentioned journalists and industry professionals in Yugoslavia immediately began to discuss the Delta achievement, they were forced to give him the telegram so he would not learn about his birthday present afterward, from the newspapers he read every morning.

Most of the professional public praised and supported the presented achievement and could not deny that a lot of domestic knowledge and work was built into the computer; even the offended republican and federal politicians were careful in their statements and did not call the leadership of Delta and Elektrotehna to account for their actions. Because of the determination of Delta employees and the speed and spontaneity of the events, the political representatives, still recovering from their shock, mostly praised the achievement of Delta, even in front of journalists. And these, in turn, also because of the way their surprised editors behaved toward the unusual gift to Tito, went on to publish everything important about the opening; this made it possible for the achievement to be published in all major Yugoslav newspapers and, thereby, Delta garnered some fantastic free advertising.

There was no doubt that Delta would never be able to obtain a license to produce if the presentation had not been successful. Specific electronics manufacturers tied to politics in Yugoslavia, through their connections, would have prevented the presentation of the Delta computer and, with it, the granting of the status of manufacturer to Elektrotehna-Delta.

They would have had another reason, as some large companies in the electronics industry of Yugoslavia had already purchased licenses from the U.S. companies for the production of computer models that were already intended to cease production and sales in the U.S. market due to their noncompetitiveness. License agreements were signed for the assembly of the originally imported computers in one location for the needs of all Yugoslav users.

This production agreement did not project any involvement for Yugoslav-made assemblies or sub-assemblies and only allowed the Yugoslav-licensed partner the development of specific applications for business programs, which the foreign licensor did not have the opportunity to develop due to the specific Yugoslav legislation. For the money the licensor received from the Yugoslav partner, they only had to educate the appropriate number of partner engineers to manage the installation and maintenance of the computer, so that the licensor mainly made net earnings by selling the license. The Yugoslav electronics manufacturers, due to very bad license agreements they signed mainly with Americans, could not successfully compete with Delta to win the Yugoslav market. Due to the large losses they had in this business, most of them eventually dropped out.

# Chapter 6

# Formation of Iskra Delta

For Delta, the computer presentation marked the beginning of the crucial period to prove itself as a producer. First, it had to solve spatial problems, which were acute due to its rapid growth. With the help of local government in Ljubljana, it was able to renovate a bigger cellar more quickly, which was then converted into a production workshop with only the essential equipment needed to start production in smaller quantities. It also had to source and ensure quality domestic suppliers of sub-assemblies: cabinets for installation of computer components, rectifiers, and power and cooling units. Delta also had to sign relevant agreements with the original U.S. and Japanese manufacturers of disk drives, tape drives, and printers.

Some of these specialized manufacturers of computer peripheral units were also suppliers for DEC, so the choices in such cases were easier for Delta.

In establishing business contacts with specialized producers who had even more favourable prices, Delta helped itself by sending only the best experts to exchange knowledge with the chosen suppliers with the task of trying to find out what the latest developments were in a particular computer field in the world, particularly with the manufacturers of compatible DEC equipment.

Such valuable knowledge was most successfully gained by experts at the beginning, who were sent to school, for example, for disk control units to the manufacturer System Industries in Santa Clara, U.S. It did not take long for them to find out that the control units of this manufacturer were already quite old and they would only waste time and company money at that school. They were fortunate enough to meet other students there who told about other producers of DEC equipment. They took advantage of the opportunity of living and networking in Silicon Valley, the core of the computer development industry in the U.S. at the time. In consultation with company management, they organized their office in the hotel; from there, they created connections with other leading U.S. companies, such as Ampex and National Semiconductor.

They also discovered that there were significantly more producers of compatible equipment that had a more modern design, and used significantly newer essential components, superior in the price-performance ratio than those Delta had used in its early production. They resorted to tricks, asking producers of the control units about the most advanced computer peripheral equipment, such as disk drives, tape drives, and line printers, and vice versa; they learned from the manufacturers of peripheral units about the best producers of control units for their products. In this way, they came to the best and most competitive suppliers for the production program at Delta, which were based on DEC processors. The contract with the companies in the wood industry, which exported to the U.S., was also very important. These contracts allowed Delta to purchase of foreign currency, to which these companies had the right at the time.

Delta reduced its own input by reducing the import component, so they could pay more to the wood companies for foreign currencies, and these companies were, therefore, able to increase their exports. This cooperation was mutually beneficial; politicians on the side of dedicated producers could not easily stop it, although they still tried in every possible way.

Intertrade company, the Yugoslav representative of IBM, also tried to prevent Delta's operation in all possible ways, and at that time had by far the largest market share in sales of computers in Yugoslavia. Since IBM computers were the most expensive, they started losing customers with the

Delta's aggressive onset. Delta started to introduce its own minicomputers, little-known at the time, that were compatible with DEC minicomputers. They were simpler and equally powerful but much cheaper than IBM's. Intertrade started to lose a lot of business with IBM computers, as companies paid half as much for Delta computers of around the same performance because of not previously having to provide foreign currency in Belgrade for imports.

Regardless of the pricing policy at that time, Delta earned a lot, and, therefore, rapidly developed and expanded, which gave rise to much envy in Yugoslavia. With its entrepreneurial activity, which was not allowed, they were causing problems for the political leadership, and they in turn were not accustomed to anyone else working in their own way. Additionally, they were developing quite rapidly and had been founded without a plan, without the leadership's permission.

Special high pressure was put on the political representatives of companies who had previously purchased a license to manufacture computers and spent state foreign currency funds, but did not have anything to show other than complete licensing imports of computers that also happened to be much more expensive than Delta's computers, even without the domestic value added. The army then played an important role in a decision by the federal government to begin manufacturing computers in Yugoslavia; the representatives saw an increasing number of computers used for different purposes, particularly in weapons systems in the armies of the Western countries. Because of the importance of the Yugoslav military and its industry, which was a major exporter of arms to the Non-Aligned countries, the army wanted to have a computer genuinely made in Yugoslavia which would contain a minimum of imported components.

The Department of Informatics within the army, therefore, decided to assemble a committee of their experts with the task of visiting all the companies of the Yugoslav electronic industry that could be responsible for the development of a Yugoslav computer, including Delta. When discussing the modernization of the army at one of the Army meetings, Tito actually asked what had happened to the computer those boys had made for his birthday. Because of Tito's interest, they did not dare to exclude Delta from the list of potential manufacturers. This commission made unannounced visits to all the companies that claimed to be manufacturing home computers, but, fortunately for Delta, they mainly found still-packaged components of imported computers. They did not find any signs of production at any of the companies indebted with the government, let alone their own development.

The visit of this committee was decisive, although they were not prepared for it. Delta already had a modest production set-up in the renovated basement of the adapted boiler room, as well as certain components that were developed and put into manufacture, such as electronic components for controlling computer peripherals, and appropriate software. The development had its own computer memory unit on the basis of memory components that could be purchased in the East, as well. A key issue was that the cabinet computers with power and cooling parts were already developed and manufactured at Delta cooperators in Slovenia.

After the visit, the committee, in its report, wrote that only Delta did not import complete computers, that they were the only ones already developing and producing certain components of the computer and that, given the knowledge and the development orientation of their engineers, they had a real chance to become, if well linked to the existing domestic electronics industry, the producer of computers for the Army's needs, as well. On the basis of this report, the backdoor industry and political games of how to prevent Delta from developing into an appreciable computer manufacturer and provider of integrated solutions for automation of company and institution management abruptly stopped.

This report was also given to the government of the Republic of Slovenia and, to protect the bad moves made by the influential Slovenian companies by purchasing licenses, it adopted legislation under which all companies that wanted to work in the field of computer manufacturing in Slovenia had to connect. Since, in Slovenia, two large manufacturers, Gorenje and Iskra, were battling over which should be the producer and developer in Slovenia, the republic government decided that Delta should become an organization of special social significance with the mission of connecting all facilities in the area of computer science in Slovenia. Delta, therefore, at the behest of the republic's policy, split from Elektrotehna in accordance with its then self-managing legislation and began to associate with Gorenje and Iskra.

Gorenje was very ambitious in expanding its programs. They commissioned a study on how seriously to enter the world of electronics and informatics at the faculty of electrical engineering at the end of the seventies. They had a few good staff in the field of consumer electronics, and in the program in the field of electronics, they had their production of televisions in Velenje and later their factory for television production in Körting, Germany. The study, among other things, also provided the opportunity to enter the field of microelectronics, and on this basis, they started talks with various potential licensors, including the Japanese Fujitsu, which was in its development heavily dependent on the U.S. computer company Amdahl. They never entered the field of microelectronics, and the talks on the planned entry into computer science with various American giants proved fruitless.

But Iskra was a vertically organized corporation with its own production of electronic components, assemblies, and even some systems. They produced the telecommunications systems to equip homes and businesses, specializing in telecommunications systems for energy, railways, highways, and public telecommunications networks. They also produced automation systems for railways, for the regulation of traffic in cities, telecommunications and laser systems for military purposes, etc. In addition to this, they were a very important producer of electric motors, relays and precision assemblies, and components.

The number of employees had grown to 33,000, of which about 3000 were highly educated, 2000 were scholarship fellows in regular education programs, and 2000 employees were being educated during work.

Iskra exports during those years reached 220 million USD. Of this, 75 million was achieved in the developed Western countries, 61 million in developing countries, and 84 million in the Soviet Union and other Eastern countries.

Iskra opened its own factory with microelectronic circuits with 5 micron C-mos technology in 1982, which produced domestically developed integrated circuits after the technological licensing of the U.S. company AMI.

Due to technological and political supremacy of Iskra over Gorenje, Delta was renamed as Iskra Delta. According to its strategy and development orientation, and by joining Iskra, Delta immediately acquired the potential opportunity to use Iskra's productive and technological capacities, especially in the fields of microelectronics, optics, and telecommunications, which represented a synergistic development priority regarding development of information technology at that time in the world. They gained access to other corporate systems, such as the Institute for Quality and Metrology, the IN-DOC system and the corporate library, the patent office, and the house training system.

The biggest problem for Iskra Delta was the fact that they also had to include in their organization those computer science-related units from Iskra and Gorenje, which, due to covering their losses, had a financially crippling and bad impact on Delta and partly hampered their development. This inorganic, forced expansion, with more than 500 new employees, caused Iskra Delta not only financial, but also major structural, personnel, and organizational problems in the beginning. With this move, some in Slovenia deliberately wanted to slow down the company because they did not believe that Delta would be able to solve existing problems without the involvement of state policy and without the promised financial assistance from the state.

To further complicate this situation, the republic's leadership, immediately after the inclusion of Delta into Iskra, appointed to the position of Vice-President of the Federal Chamber of Commerce in Belgrade the then-president of Iskra, who prioritized Iskra's overall interests and saw in the inclusion a large, positive momentum of continued strategic development for Iskra as a whole.

Later, it turned out that this staff move was a good move because he made an important contribution to the new function, allowing the federal government to keep the agreement with the U.S. government concerning the export of Yugoslav products, which included the latest U.S. technology, to countries that were under the U.S. embargo.

Iskra Delta leaders, due to such interference of policy, found themselves in considerable difficulty, for they knew they were the only ones to bear responsibility for any failure to integrate parts of Iskra and Gorenje into Iskra Delta, and politics would be clean of its wrong decisions in this way, decisions which Iskra Delta was warned of upon its forced and abnormal formation. With great efforts of all the employees, the integration was successfully executed in the shortest possible time and with costs that Iskra Delta could cover from their current operations.

This happened primarily through innovation and new organization, in which the joined units from Iskra and Gorenje immediately got their place and duties. It was necessary to change the work schedule for the newly-acquired workers and keep them fully employed, and to integrate the creative staff as soon as possible into development projects that were already running or being implemented at that time.

With the experts of the joined Iskra Tozd computers who already had experience in the development and production of microcomputers, they immediately set up a separate program, which soon put new products on the market, among which the computers Partner and Triglav were the most successful.

The new organization was characterized by income and cost independent programs, was responsible for developing and manufacturing various types of computers and for the sales applicative branches, and was responsible for developing and introducing the most comprehensive software solutions for specific sectors of the economy. This organization allowed the organizational units a high degree of self-initiative regarding interest integration in both the manufacturers of the electronic sub-assemblies as well as with the leading media technology solutions for individual economic and social activities throughout Yugoslavia.

The management of Iskra Delta paid particular attention to its presence throughout the Yugoslav market from the very beginning of its development. Iskra Delta, therefore, had its own sales service centres in all major cities in the republics of the former Yugoslavia, in Belgrade, Zagreb, Sarajevo, Skopje, Novi Sad, Split, Rijeka, and Maribor, where the employees were locals who were logically the easiest to connect with the domestic economy. This had important significance for success in the market and the formation of applicative branches.

From the outset, its sales policy was based on as close integration with the users as was possible. This proved successful in deflecting attacks from foreign computer firms. In contrast, the agents of foreign, mainly U.S., firms behaved arrogantly toward their customers in Yugoslavia because they were convinced that international buyers must adapt to them and not vice versa. They believed that Iskra Delta, with its approach, tiny size, and insignificance in the world, would not withstand the pressure for long; although its image was in fact covertly organized for this effect.

Notwithstanding these efforts to attain the best results in Yugoslavia, the management was aware that there could be no assurance of stable development without insurance of their own foreign currency funds for imports of essential components for the production of various models of computers. This could be achieved only through the export of their products and services. Opponents knew that the most vulnerable spot in its development was in the provision of necessary foreign currency funds for imports of computer components and sub-assemblies from the U.S. and Japan, because the company was dependent on the purchase of foreign currencies at higher prices from their partners, particularly the wood industry, one of the few net exporters in Yugoslavia at the time.

By early 1980, they had set up their representative office in New York and were offering their development products and services to the demanding U.S. market. This office also had great importance in establishing business contacts with the U.S. suppliers and for searching for subcontractors and development partners. Through self-representation, they stayed informed in the best possible way of the latest developments in Silicon Valley, primarily with the emerging companies in information technology, which at that time represented the biggest driving force of development, such as Microsoft. Their representative bought the right to use that operating software for Delta's multiprocessor computer, Trident. At the time of this purchase, Microsoft was smaller than Iskra Delta.

Delta's field of export to the Soviet Union and other Eastern countries, located in Novi Sad, was very successful. The problem of exports to the East at the time was that they did not receive payments in foreign currency but mainly in convertible minerals, which was a very lucrative income but required additional commercial efforts to transform into the needed foreign currencies. They also had a special system of rewarding employees, according to the success of the program or branch and the results for the quarter. This, at that time, was a considerable novelty in Yugoslavia. The ability to include the best experts from all over Yugoslavia into Iskra Delta and to directly motivate employees was very much related to the success of individual organizational units and enterprises as a whole, and provided faster development and superior business results, among the best in former Yugoslavia.

For even faster development, setting up the organization of applicative branches for individual sectors of the economy in the individual republics was very important, as were their relationships with companies that were the most technologically advanced in their activities. Such an approach was unique at that time in the world.

The branches were:

- Energy and mining
- Banking and insurance
- Industry
- Agriculture and food industry
- Construction and design
- Tourism and hospitality
- Commerce
- Medicine
- State administration

Not only were experts in the field of computer science employed, but also, experts in various fields were covered by the branches in such a manner that they could offer complete turnkey solutions with the knowledge of technological and organizational processes to users in these areas.

Such policies enabled, for example, the Energy branch, which was formed when the company Energy Systems merged with Iskra Delta, to produce and implement the complete project management and automation of power plants and other energy facilities, among which were also Electro Istria Pula and one of the largest hydroelectric plants Europe, HP Đerdap, on the Danube River in Serbia, with an installed capacity of more than 1000 MW. This was possible for the Energy branch primarily because of their own developed electronic sub-assemblies and SCADA software package adapted by their engineers to the widest possible use in process engineering in conjunction with technology partner Landis&Gyr in Switzerland.

In 1984, they were among the first in the world to carry out the project of IT management and remote management of hydroelectric power. This project was realized at the hydroelectric plant Solkan on the river Soča, with an installed power of 31 MW and an annual output of 110,000 MWh of electricity. This power is operated and managed from the control centre several kilometres away, in Nova Gorica, and in the initial ten-year period, the operations and management worked with 99.4 percent reliability.

The Iskra Delta management attributed great importance to the education of both employees and users of its computers from the outset. Their engineers received basic skills training at DEC. With the rapid development and the substantial needs of the users of their computers for new knowledge, quality education was essential, but educating abroad was not the most economical, due to high costs. In line with its development strategy, the management made a timely decision to establish its own training centre, in which some of their overseas trained professionals became the first lecturers. In an atmosphere of awareness of the critical importance of education for further development, they sought different solutions and options to significantly increase their own education. They needed a location that could provide excellent conditions for all-day education, that would have a hotel close by, a computer centre equipped with computers, and large classrooms with terminals at each the table.

In early 1984, the head of the business unit in Nova Gorica introduced the idea to buy the defunct hotel Argonauts in Nova Gorica and arrange an educational centre there. The idea was very bold for those times. This was a complex consisting of almost two hectares of land, a hotel with over 100 rooms and more than 10,000 square meters of covered area, in the centre of Nova Gorica, near the country's border with Italy. The director, accustomed to bold ideas, immediately called for the high-level staff to carefully study the idea. In a very short time, the decision was made that this was the only chance at that moment for Iskra Delta's development; it was not very favourable, but they would have the necessary facilities for a comprehensive and modern training centre sooner rather than later. All employees involved in the realization of these ideas acted in a very coordinated and quick fashion because this was the only way they could effectively exploit the collapsing Argonauts Hotel for the good of Iskra Delta. This hotel, due to structural defects, had begun disintegrating during the original construction project, so local politicians offered it to Delta on the condition that they renovate it as soon as possible.

The ruins of this hotel were on the border with Italy and represented a cultural shame for Yugoslavia, so the matter of a speedy renovation was important; in support of this, the local and republic's politicians did everything in their power to assist Iskra Delta to quickly acquire the appropriate financial credits and any necessary administrative consent for change of use, and for the construction itself. This allowed them to fix the decaying facility in a record time of just one year and to reconfigure it into a modern educational centre with adjoining hotel, providing a good standard for students to learn and stay under one roof at a unique location.

In parallel with the construction of the building itself, the experts of Iskra Delta also produced an equipment plan, similar to IBM and DEC school centres. This training centre was, therefore, at the opening in early 1985, one of the most modern and best equipped in Europe, and gave Iskra Delta further impetus for development. It was important that existing and prospective customers feel sure of the capabilities and knowledge of their experts. They could organize seminars and demonstrate their system and application solutions in the centre's well-equipped rooms and classrooms, fitted out with video terminals and other cutting-edge equipment.

This centre became a major research and technological centre for information technology in the former Yugoslavia and the heart of Iskra Delta's development itself. It was also important as a demonstration centre for its products and solutions, as, there, they could present the most demanding design and simulation tasks, which mainly were requested by representatives of major users. They usually wanted specific turnkey solutions that Iskra Delta had to do, which only the U.S. companies were able to do at the time. The centre's services were also gradually beginning to be used by their suppliers in such a way that their experts from the U.S. educated Iskra Delta engineers there.

DEC gave a lot of recognition to Iskra Delta and their educational centre when their representatives took a look at it and saw what Iskra Delta had made without their direct assistance. Eventually, DEC also started to provide specific education for end users of their computers in Yugoslavia there. Representatives of other countries soon began to take interest in the activities at the centre, and among the first important foreign officials to visit the centre was the Indian Ambassador; this took place shortly after the opening, at his own request. Iskra Delta realized the importance of this visit only when they received tempting offers to cooperate with the Indian government.

Due to the rapid development and growth, Iskra Delta had great difficulty in providing spatial developmental production capacities at that time, largely because its development production facilities were scattered around the republic in Ljubljana, Kranj, Velenje, and Ptuj, which caused additional costs and was not the most economical operation. In these plants, they produced DEC-compatible minicomputers, Partner and Triglav personal computers, video terminals, electronic assemblies, and integrated circuits.

Management was aware that rapid growth was no longer possible without new, modern development of Iskra Delta's production capacity. In a timely manner and according to their own project plans, they prepared a new factory in Ljubljana, for which it was necessary to obtain the appropriate permits and long-term financial assets, none of which was possible without the consent of the political authorities in the republic. These were facts that were used by opponents of Iskra Delta and competing foreign computer companies through their representatives in Yugoslavia.

The most active, in particular, were the IBM representatives, who began lobbying politicians on the grounds that Iskra Delta did not need such facilities because they would not be able to follow the future of development, which would be dictated by IBM. These representatives were aware that the growth of Iskra Delta and its capacity would bring more losses to their business in Yugoslavia. They were concerned about the loss of high incomes the most, which was made possible by the sales of large IBM computers, which were, compared with Delta computers, expensive and, moreover, required expensive maintenance and had high operating costs.

Due to strong competitive pressures and opponents of the development within Iskra itself, Iskra Delta's management had to find its own solutions and obtain funds through advanced payments from its customers and at a higher interest rate on the grey financial market. It obtained the greatest credit for the realization of the construction project of the new development production capacities from its chosen investment provider, which began work on Iskra Delta's behalf and for its own benefit, but which came from another republic; therefore, the works could start sooner than the formal approval was obtained.

When its opponents in Slovenia realized they could not prevent Iskra Delta's investment in new facilities by manipulating administrative difficulties, they tried to replace Iskra Delta's leadership by placing the Iskra leadership under an expedited procedure in early 1987 on the grounds that it did not properly follow the development policies of Iskra, causing Iskra problems throughout its development. In doing so, they went so far as using supporters in Slovenian politics to influence the banks in Slovenia to block Iskra Delta's payment of salaries. They believed the workers themselves would change the leadership if salaries were not paid on time. This would happen only if the leadership did not obtain the support of the majority of workers in time.

Fortunately, political organizations in Iskra Delta and, subsequently, those at the top of the Yugoslav Army, which due to foreign interests in their products and their own development plans, which included Iskra Delta, stepped in to help at the right time. Since the opponents were unaware of these relationships and had also underestimated the determination of Iskra Delta's leadership, their attempts ended in failure, and Iskra Delta managed to realize its new production capabilities at the end of 1987, albeit with great sacrifices in its technical and market development. The opening of the new development production facilities, which were at that time the most modern and best equipped for development and production of complex products in the field of information technology in Europe, was attended by the president of the Republic Committee for Science and Technology, the president of the Slovenian Academy of Sciences and Arts, and the rector of the University of Ljubljana.

Journalists attended in great numbers from all over Yugoslavia and reported on the huge success of Iskra Delta, which embarrassed the leading politicians considerably for their failure to participate in the opening of the latest and largest centre for developing and manufacturing high technology products in former Yugoslavia. Some representatives from the opposition to Iskra Delta's development were also present, praising the achievement with their fingers crossed in their pockets because they did not want to admit temporary defeat of their struggle in public, which they led at the behest of foreigners, hampering the development of Iskra Delta, hoping to gradually lead to its liquidation.

The result of the battle for new capacities and domestic intrigue left Iskra Delta exhausted. The company was paying insufficient attention to the rapid development of microcomputers, which were reaching their maximum development and the widest scope of use exactly at that time. At the beginning, Iskra Delta was successfully catching up to this development with the multifunctional computer Triglav (Trident), which at its presentation was one of the most modern in the world. In part due to this success, also foreigners began taking Iskra Delta seriously. Through their allies in Iskra and in the political arena, the opponents wanted to prevent the timely start of Trident's mass production and thus prevent

Iskra Delta from becoming an important player in the global field, which was dominated by the U.S. firms.

IBM, through their representative Intertrade, went so far as to offer to another company within Iskra to manufacture their own PC, if the leadership of Iskra would disable the leadership of Iskra Delta. Quick presentations of Trident abroad, mainly in London and in Germany, and a prize for the best product at a fair in Germany, prevented this from happening immediately.

The biggest surprise came from the Mercedes Development Institute company in Germany, with the purchase of forty Trident computers. This shut the mouths of the opponents, mostly in Slovenia, who had long proclaimed, according to instructions from abroad, that Iskra Delta could not compete with the American companies in information technologies with their own development. This success knocked an important weapon out of the opponents' hands because the Mercedes name was so highly regarded that they could not belittle Iskra Delta's position on the international market.

An important factor in the surging development of Iskra Delta at that time was their ability to put their development achievements into production and on the market relatively rapidly. This was quite unusual under the conditions in Yugoslavia at the time.

To enhance their performance on the market, they took advantage of specialized fairs in Ljubljana and Zagreb as much as possible. Interbiro, at the fairgrounds in Zagreb, was especially important, as customers attended not only from Yugoslavia, but also from the east and from the non-aligned countries. To be able to show all their products and services, in particular the latest developments in the field of connecting computers to networks, Iskra Delta rented the entire Austrian pavilion at the Zagreb fairgrounds as early as the fair in 1984.

This move brought great commercial success, since for the first time, customers could see their entire range of products in one place. With the displayed products and services, Iskra

Delta was not behind anyone; they represented a huge surprise, as visitors could see the solutions and products, which even the U.S. companies could not present at the fair. In fairness, this was largely due to the restrictive U.S. government policies on exports of the latest technologies. Still, the abilities of Iskra Delta were exhibited in a larger room at this event than the giant IBM.

They caused interest even with the representatives of the largest countries that were not in NATO, especially the Soviet Union, China, and India. Even representatives of the Yugoslav government and military came to realize that this company, formed in such a short time, was producing products and services that inspired respect and interest from the most important countries. Relevant departments of the Yugoslav government subsequently began to monitor it more closely, soon joining the game of other foreign intelligence services, something no one at Iskra Delta knew at the time.

During this period of the Cold War, technological advantages of the West were beginning to show the most. In limited armed conflicts, especially in the Middle East, the American allies with weapons systems based on information technology overcame enemies armed with Soviet weapons systems like cutting through a piece of cake. In these conflicts, it was clearly shown that the most advanced information management technologies were crucial; something that was realized too late in the East, so naturally they tried to catch up. With a cruel realization, they endeavoured with accelerated efforts and resorted to stealing Western technology.

Another important operation of Iskra Delta delivering a breakthrough on the market and its international exposure was the focus on producing a solution for computer monitoring of sporting events. In the beginning, it was especially used for winter sports such as ski jumping in Planica and alpine skiing in Kranjska Gora. In this area, they broke new ground, since there were few computer companies at the end of the seventies willing and able to process real-time data at similar events.

That was why they were entrusted with the data processing at that time in international competitions in the following events:

- Marathons in Slovenia—ski and summer from 1980 to 1989
- Ski jumping—the world cup on Planica from 1979 to 1989
- Ski races in the Alpine disciplines—Kranjska Gora and Maribor
- World Cup, Kranjska Gora –1984, 1985, 1986
- World Cup, Maribor –1984, 1985, 1986
- Winter Universiade—Czechoslovakia, 1987
- Athletics—Balkan Championship, Ljubljana, September 1986
- World Rowing Championships, Bled, September 1989.

In these competitions, Iskra Delta carried out full IT support, which included the installation of the mainframe computer with many terminals for accreditation of journalists, records of all participants and the collection, and distribution of results at various locations.

Processing of results in real time and continuous data transfer between the core computers was usually carried out through a network of Partner microcomputers, which were connected with Longines clocks and a graphic character generator to control a large scoreboard where the results were shown. Their display was made available on printers installed in the commentary booths and at the press centre.

# Chapter 7

# Iskra Delta Establishes its Business Unit in the U.S. and Branches Out to Austria

Iskra Delta executives came to the realization in 1983 that by only developing in Yugoslavia, they would not be able to compete with computer companies in the West. They decided to establish their companies there, instead, in accordance with the legislation of the time. Not long after, Iskra Delta opened its specialized unit within the Iskra company, which had an office in New York and a branch in Santa Clara, California. The following year, they founded their own company, Iskra Delta Computers (IDC), in Austria, based in Klagenfurt.

One of the main tasks of the unit in the U.S. was getting technology partners to buy specifically developed electronic sub-assemblies and software from Iskra Delta for use in market niches for special applications with the U.S. buyers who used microcomputers based on Intel and Motorola microprocessors. The unit in Santa Clara, in the famous Silicon Valley, also had an important role in the purchase of electronic components and sub-assemblies as well as system software[22] and technological equipment for development and production in Yugoslavia.

It was especially important in this unit that the Iskra Delta engineers who came from Yugoslavia could immediately test the home-developed electronic modules. This was made possible by easy access to cutting-edge development equipment,

---

[2]An example of this activity was the porting of the operating system Unix for Intel's 32-bit processor in Trident, one of the first in the world.

Trident Iskra Delta multiprocessor system

which was then mainly developed and manufactured by the companies in Silicon Valley. Therefore, they could easily complete the development of their own, home-based Trident system (Triglav) on this unit, which was a state of the art technology product in its class in the world at that time.

The head of this unit had an important role, particularly in making contacts with the then-rapidly emerging U.S. IT companies such as Motorola, Intel, Microsoft, and Digital Research, from which Iskra Delta purchased microprocessors and operating system software for their Partner microcomputer and later for their multiprocessor system, Trident. Because of the leading role Digital Research held before Microsoft in operating software, Iskra Delta bought their operating system software, CP/M, instead of the Microsoft MS/DOS in the belief that Digital Research would prevail in the area of operating systems for personal computers in the world and become a global standard.

This purchase was a big strategic mistake that resulted in Iskra Delta developing their applicative programs in an operating system which was incompatible with IBM PCs, which operated on the basis of MS/DOS after Microsoft had entered into a large-scale contract with IBM. Due to their mass production and their position in the market, IBM soon established Microsoft MS/DOS as the standard for use and development of applicative business programs for personal computers in the world instead of CP/M.

Due to its presence in Silicon Valley and the potential for contacting the then-leading companies in the development and production of IT equipment in the world, Iskra Delta could immediately make products that competed with the best in the West. The unfriendly environment for the development and production of high-tech products in Yugoslavia encouraged it to take a further step and transfer part of its activities for the demanding Western markets directly to the West.

This was done by setting up a company in Austria which had its head office and sales in Klagenfurt. The development and training centre was on the site of the Hotel Korotan at Wörthersee, which they bought together with the land, and the production of complex electronic modules was organized in rented premises in Šentjakob, not far from the border.

Iskra Delta decided to transfer, first and foremost, the further development and production of the Trident computer to Austria, because it was intended for sale primarily in the western market due to its competitiveness and innovative technology solutions. This move had great strategic importance since it made it easier to purchase the modern technological development equipment and computer components in the U.S. and, at the same time, avoided any import administrative obstacles in the country. Computers manufactured in Austria got the status of the products in the developed West, which was very important for selling to Western countries.

In the West, people could not believe that a company in a country like Yugoslavia was manufacturing such high-level technology products as personal computers and advanced workstations with developed graphical user interfaces. Basically everything the Trident system consisted of was fully developed by Iskra Delta engineers, for which they received a special republic award for inventions and improvements.

# DIPLOM

TRIGLAV – TRIDENT

DEM AUF DER LEIPZIGER

FRÜHJAHRSMESSE 1987

AUSGESTELLTEN ERZEUGNIS

WIRD IN ANERKENNUNG

HERVORRAGENDER QUALITÄT

DIE GOLDMEDAILLE

ZUERKANNT UND

DEM AUSSTELLER

Iskra Delta Computers,

DIESES DIPLOM ÜBERREICHT

LEIPZIG, DEN 15 MÄRZ 1987

AMT FÜR STANDARDISIERUNG, MESSWESEN
UND WARENPRÜFUNG
DER PRÄSIDENT

LEIPZIGER MESSAMT
DER GENERALDIREKTOR

Gold medal for Trident on international fair in Germany

A patent application was also made for the original solutions, as the system allowed the exchange of different process modules, configuration of different computers, and use both in the business as well as in process applications.

The Trident system had, among other things, the following features and capabilities:

- For the time, a unique 32-bit universal guidance with address and data support
- Selection of processors
  - Intel 80386
  - Motorola MC 68010
  - DEC DC J11-AC
- Selection of operating systems
  - OS 9
  - DELTA/M
  - IRMX from Intel
  - UNIX and XENIX;
- Support of 2D and 3D graphical interface with colour graphics
- Multiprocessor operation
- Different interfaces for peripheral units
- Interfaces for real-time process control

The Universal Applicability of the Trident

Due to its unique design, the Trident was aimed at different customers in the global technology summit, which gave it a great advantage in the market at that time over other computer systems that were similar. This is why it won the gold medal at the Leipzig Fair in Germany. It could be configured for various uses:

- Workstation in design studios
- Graphic working site for CAD design
- Intelligent terminal for larger computers
- Work node in the Delta net network
- Integrated workplace for business purposes

There was also a special miniature version of Trident for use in weapons systems based on a flexible WME. This was presented as the Trident-Piccolo on the market.

Iskra Delta could compete using their computer system Trident at that time with the most demanding computers in their class, most of which were made in Silicon Valley. It had an important advantage in that it could be used for managing processes in real time as well as for business purposes, which only depended on the configuration of the computer. This configuration was simply performed while manufacturing the computer according to the customer's requirements; this in itself was an additional competitive advantage.

Because of its universal application, Iskra Delta achieved outstanding sales in Western Europe and, thus, profits. No similar product from Yugoslavia had ever reached that height in the West. Additional capacities in stock for Iskra Delta sales and faster development and production in Austria, in addition to those already mentioned, had an important impact on the employees as well, because Delta professionals could work to help their company, IDC, in Austria which had, in addition to improving productivity, generated very positive motivational and financial effects.

Development engineers accomplished achievements faster, so products passed from development into production faster. What was also important in all of this was that production, service, and sales documentation of the developed product was on time, so that IDC in Austria really could respond immediately to special customer requirements, which was a great advantage over similar U.S. companies, and created for itself a profitable market niche for its introduction on the Western market, where the U.S. computer companies had the controlling voice. The effect could be seen in development costs, since Iskra Delta could quickly hire labour-saving development and production equipment, which was not easy in Yugoslavia because of the rigid laws and the chronic shortage of foreign exchange.

Obtaining additional space for user training, which Iskra Delta acquired by buying the Korotan Hotel, had proven to be a very good move because the buyers who were unable or unwilling to come to school in Yugoslavia could acquire this knowledge in Austria, which had a special, more open status in the West. This status was also important for buyers from the East, as well as for those from the Western countries. Buyers from Eastern countries especially liked to attend seminars in Western countries, as they could get special permission to go to the West for this purpose but not as tourists. This training centre complemented the one in Nova Gorica very well, giving Iskra Delta an additional impetus for development and international importance that no one at home or abroad had anticipated.

# Chapter 8

## The Trident Multiprocessor Computer Presentation in London and the PARSYS Project at the Main Development Institutes in the U.S. and Japan

The successful and highly acclaimed presentation of the Trident (Triglav) computer in London to the professional public and journalists was important to the further rapid and unobstructed development of Iskra Delta. Its leadership had to follow suit because of the need for convertible foreign currency, more necessary each day due to the rapid development and increasing production of computer equipment. Inflows from foreign exchange arranged by the wood industry were no longer sufficient; therefore, it was necessary to acquire it by selling Iskra Delta's products and services directly in the developed Western market. According to the former Yugoslav law, companies could use earned foreign currencies to import reproduction material from the West according to their needs.

Trident, which Iskra Delta produced in its company in Austria, was well received by the demanding test customers in Germany, which was crucial in the management's decision to pay the substantial financial costs for the promotion and sales activities of Trident and its software solutions for a wide range of applications, even to customers in the wider

Western market. Trident was the result of this development and had the highest added value. Given its competitive price in the market, it also implied substantial earnings.

As the starting point for sales activities of Trident in the West, they chose the complex and large markets of West Germany and Great Britain. The Trident presentation in London was instructive for the public; they also made sure to invite some renowned British retailers of computer equipment. Equally instructive was the press conference for British journalists. The response to the invitation was small, as expected; it seemed illogical to the British that a high tech product could come from undeveloped Yugoslavia at that time. Certain retailers and journalists nevertheless accepted the invitation, though, as they later said, more out of curiosity to find out how the Yugoslavs had masked the American computer in order to be able to sell it as their own.

The Trident presentation in London was held by the head manager and his colleagues, who had played an important role in the development and preparation of sales documentation for the Trident. They arrived at the presentation in London in a specially adapted small plane so they could smoothly bring in some Trident computers already configured for different applications and some of the key components developed and produced by Iskra Delta.

When the attending British saw the Trident computers and their components, they could not believe that they were designed, developed, and made in a Balkan country. They were even more surprised when it was demonstrated exactly what these computers could do. Trident was then one of the few computers in the world which could work with three different processors and three operating systems. It, therefore, had a very wide range of applications. Nobody expected such capabilities; the British were truly stunned, much to the satisfaction of those who had anticipated such a response when preparing for this event in Ljubljana.

They allowed everybody present to realize for themselves the truth about the Trident's remarkable operation, as this was their first step in reaching out and touching an unfamiliar audience. If they had only revealed promotional documentation without the product being present, no one would believe that what was presented was made in Yugoslavia. There were even people who demanded that the attending experts open the Trident so they could be sure that it was really made from the key components made by Iskra Delta. They were particularly impressed by the modern form and design and the practical configuration options for different applications, a significant advantage for sales to demanding customers in Western Europe.

Only when they were satisfied that everything Iskra Delta meant to sell in Britain was really made in Yugoslavia, meaning in its factories in Slovenia and Austria, they listened with interest to the presentation and started spontaneously to engage in discussion. First, they wanted to know as much as possible about Iskra Delta and Slovenia. When the director explained to them that it was founded similarly to the related companies in Silicon Valley and developed into an information technology company without government support, they simply could not comprehend how that was possible in Communist Yugoslavia. The ice was broken; a lot of technical questions began to be posed, and the attending representatives of commercial companies started to show interest in selling products and representing Iskra Delta in the UK market.

The presentation started to be what Iskra Delta imagined. Many hardware vendors quickly realized that what they saw in front of them were highly marketable products, so they called in their own companies' experts to come and see the amazing computer products from Yugoslavia. The head manager of Iskra Delta invited representatives of companies who showed interest in the sale of the Trident in the UK and other Western countries to indicate their demand in writing and not to overlook the fact that they would have to take into account the conditions that were placed in the sales documentation, as well as the fact that they would then represent Iskra Delta in the agreed markets.

His confident performance at the presentation of the sales conditions and pre-sales documentation further convinced the British retailers that Iskra Delta had ultimately realized the value of its Trident system; they knew what they wanted and did not intend to sell it at lower prices just because it came from Yugoslavia instead of the U.S. Managers at Iskra Delta also read good knowledge into the situation on the Western market, where the U.S. computers dominated; they knew exactly which market niche these products were intended for. At the presentation of the Trident, the head manager did not avoid comparison with the most competitive U.S. computers, clearly identifying the degree of performance and how competitive the price was. The present expert gave convincing answers to questions about the quality and warranty conditions and stated that they would undoubtedly be, according to their years of experience working with U.S. computer firms and providing service for the DEC computers, providing quality and warranties for their Trident computers similar to what the American manufacturers provided for their computers.

The result of such an approach was visible shortly after the introductory commercial talks when one of the attending retailers offered to buy one of the exhibited Trident computers on the spot, to pay in cash, and to simultaneously transport it, to ensure priority for distribution over the other attendees. Fortunately, the representatives of Iskra Delta had a response to such requests because they had prepared a document for customs, which provided an opportunity to leave some equipment in London for possible further testing and adaptation in the UK. However, they did not expect to be offered immediate payment at the distribution price, even partially in cash, which represented a particular problem. Therefore, they signed an appropriate contract with the so-called first buyer, in which they agreed to deliver the computer immediately, and the buyer would pay in full to their bank account in the normal time period. They also signed a distribution contract with this buyer before any other interested parties did so, which guaranteed an advantage.

Thus, representatives of Iskra Delta returned satisfied and without one computer; they had in fact covered the considerable costs of the presentation in London with its sale. A British journalist gave them additional free publicity in his own professional journal, where he wrote a particularly commendable story of the creation of Iskra Delta, their Trident computer, and the possibilities for further development based on strategies presented in London. On this occasion, Iskra Delta said publicly for the first time that it saw the future development of computer technology in the development of parallel processing, and the development of artificial intelligence, as well.

The ambitious development strategy made a big impression on all those present; they asked themselves with admiration and amazement how it was possible that such thinking on the future development of computer technology had come from companies in Yugoslavia, which they considered undeveloped.

The ambitious project known as PARSYS was another head-turner; it had only been linked with leading American companies and institutes until then. The parallel processing system called PARSYS was planned at Iskra Delta, and the leading institutes and development groups from different faculties in former Yugoslavia were invited to participate. The project itself required the development and manufacture of adequate prototype hardware, system software, and a special software environment for the development of application software. The PARSYS system architecture was based on 64 processors of 64 memory modules, connected through a network of steering logic units. The PARSYS system had a modular design that allowed for different configurations of the system and used 16- or 32-bit processors. As a general purpose computer system, it was designed for high speed processing in real time, especially for applications that require high processing speed, such as:

- Artificial intelligence
- Base workstations
- Database management
- Simulations
- Computer graphics
- Vision
- Structural analysis
- Aerodynamics
- Metrology
- Medical diagnosis
- Processing of sensitive signals in real time
- Genetic engineering
- Industrial and other automation and

Precisely because of the purpose of such a project, PARSYS was strategically very important, as other leading institutes and universities in the West, particularly in the U.S., had initiated similar projects. At that time, parallel processing dominated research and development in information technology. Due to its unique architecture, it was agreed among experts as the system that would best be used successfully for various types of applications, both for those written for systems based on local memory as well as for those systems based on mutually shared fast memory.

Because the PARSYS system had the capabilities of a larger computer, it held special importance. Large computers cost many millions of dollars at that time on the market, but the PARSYS system could be offered on the market for the price of a minicomputer (around ten thousand dollars) and could enable users to significantly reduce data processing costs while simultaneously and repeatedly increasing the reliability of processing. Due to the economic benefits that would result from the realization of PARSYS, Iskra Delta registered for a tender for development funding under the

European Development Project Eureka, leading to further interest of various intelligence services in its development achievements.

Because of the original design of the PARSYS project based on *hypercubes* and the initial achievements from this strategic development, the leading experts in its development soon received invitations to visit major universities and institutes in the U.S. and Japan. Visiting the leading U.S. universities and institutes such as MIT (Massachusetts Institute of Technology), Courant Institute (New York University, the developer of a parallel processor for IBM), Columbia University (NY), Carnegie Mellon University (Pittsburgh, PA), Stanford (CA), Berkeley (CA), CIT/Caltech (Pasadena, CA), Arizona University (Tucson, AZ), Purdue (IN), and Thomas J. Watson-IBM Research Center (NY) would have been impossible if Iskra Delta did not have a parallel system project of its own and a record of original achievements in this field.

At such a high level of research, emerging knowledge can only be shared; you have to give it so that you receive it in return. This is the only legitimate channel for the flow of world-class technology research information. In these first contacts between development engineers, strategic information is important: revealing novelties in a certain way, challenging with its specificity, and being critical of the existing concepts.

Exchange of information on developmental achievements of Iskra Delta was as necessary for its experts as it was for their hosts, as it needed verification of the concepts and plans of its future systems. Particularly worthy of a mention was the seminar that its experts attended in the laboratory for parallel systems at MIT and at the Courant Institute of New York University. At these, the conceptual advantage of Delta Iskra was confirmed over the so-called ultra-computer, which was a kind of prototype of the IBM parallel machine RP3.

For this reason, their hosts offered participation in development, but there were also the prejudices that always exist until concrete evidence proves the opposite. Iskra Delta experts had the opportunity to observe how these prejudices melted away as the dialogue was playing out in a professional and expert environment.[3] In such a situation, a break would occur suddenly when the hosts themselves began to offer alternatives in participation, when restrictions, bans, and embargoes fell. Only in this way, when the weaker has knowledge relevant to the stronger, is it possible to achieve respect in the early stages of such a demanding project, and with it, also, to achieve entirely equal communication.

The visit of Iskra Delta experts to the U.S. was very popular in professional circles, as it was shown that the company had the proper strategic design of development in the field of parallel computers, leading to the most important future development for mankind. This was especially true in the U.S., where there were needs for a large number of parallel computations, large amounts of data, and, of course, where there was need for great computation speed. Even then it was known at the visited institutes that these computers would be very important for developments in physics, biology, borderline interdisciplinary scientific fields, technology (complex processes, modelling, simulation and automation), and artificial intelligence. It was known that once the technology advanced, installing this parallel technology would require a large number of processors and would be possible even in personal computers.

The problem, which was then reflected, was in man and in the structure of his brain, preventing him from parallel conscious processing, for example, with parallel thinking, speaking, and listening through multiple, simultaneous channels and simultaneously perceiving multiple descriptive inputs and machinery. Such parallel functions could be almost arbitrarily complicated to organize. Even then, the direct

---

[3]The so-called PARSYS expedition delegation to the top U.S. institutes and universities in the U.S. consisted of MSc. Peter Brajak, Dr. Saša Prešern and Professor Dr. Anton P. Železnikar (Železnikar, 1987, 1988). It is interesting to note that an expedition on that level and with similarly superior research and technological content carried out in the present day would be virtually impossible.

computation speed of computers was strikingly superior compared to that of mathematicians. Therefore, just thinking about all these more powerful computers brought new perspectives and possibilities of development up to the conceptual point when computers would also be thinking.[4] This is why experts abroad were surprised when they realized that Iskra Delta's development of parallel systems included the development of a form of artificial intelligence, based on the concept of a chess game.

For an interim period in the development of new technologies, especially new components based on nano-technology, Iskra Delta developed and produced a system called GEMINI. This system was a multi-mini system created on the basis of its own experience in building parallel systems. It was designed with the standard Vax compatible processors and supported by the operating software Delta/V. It was designed primarily for those areas of work which require high reliability and complex processing.

The Gemini system was sixteen times more reliable than one processor systems at that time. More than one hundred users could have been active on it, which placed it in a highly competitive position on the market in terms of price and performance. As a result of the presentation of the system at the exhibition in Zagreb, Iskra Delta soon received many requests from Yugoslavia and abroad.

---

[4]The highest possible complexity in the number and relation of computer components, speed, and volume of storage media, and extremely flexible software and communication support will be needed in the constitution of artificial (information) awareness in the so-called spiritual machines (Kurzweil, 1999), sociable and other robotic devices (Moravec, 1999). The first embryonic ideas of the importance of meaningful information was privately presented at a private university in Stanford (Železnikar, 1987) in an interview with Professor Terry Winograd. Stanford nurtured the strict concept of information without meaning (amount of information, according to the famous concept of Shannon).

# Chapter 9

# Iskra Delta Obtains a Computer Network Project for the Chinese Police

Receiving the project for the Chinese police came as a great surprise for Iskra Delta, arriving in an unusual way for conventional business practices. It began with Iskra Delta's appearance at specialized fairs, where it raised interest from the beginning not only from domestic visitors, but also from foreigners, especially those from the Eastern Bloc, the mighty China, the Soviet Union, and the Non-Aligned countries, led by India. At these fairs, particularly at the largest specialized exhibition of this field in this part of Europe, the Interbiro in Zagreb, in addition to the products of its own development, Iskra Delta attracted much attention due to its computer presentations made following the OEM (Original Equipment Manufacturer) principle and based on DEC Vax processors. These computers contained more and more components developed each year by Iskra Delta, but they remained compatible with the original DEC computers.

After it had already decided to fully acquire the production of Vax-compatible computers, Iskra Delta executives learned that the family of these computers had become the standard for very important applications in the U.S. Army. DEC did not conceal information about this computer in the beginning. To minimize the costs of maintenance and installations in Yugoslavia, they trained the Iskra Delta engineers so well that they were doing all the work themselves.

Based on service records and knowledge obtained from DEC, Iskra Delta formed its development department with these the most qualified engineers who had the task of producing a computer processing unit based on the generic principle with a requirement that it had to be compatible with the original Vax processor. A similar plan was also prepared for both its system software and software used to connect computers to the network, because the leadership at Iskra Delta soon realized that the future of development was in network computing.

Accordingly, sales system engineers were also trained who interpreted the strategy to customers, and at fairs such as Interbiro they also demonstrated solutions which were already developed by Iskra Delta, as well as solutions offered on behalf of DEC. It was this connection between the company's own developed products and DEC's sales representative program that made a big impression on customers, because they saw that Iskra Delta engineers were proficient in demonstrating both Delta and DEC products without the assistance of DEC engineers from the U.S. or their branches in the West.

A major turning point for the interest in the products and services of Iskra Delta took place at the Interbiro Fair in Zagreb in 1984, when it came out what exactly Iskra Delta was selling at the fair as its own products and solutions, which were even more extensive than IBM. The presentation also attracted the attention of intelligence agencies, particularly those from the Eastern countries and China, as they were aware that the U.S. government prohibited exportation by companies which offered similar technology and knowledge as Iskra Delta to the countries outside NATO. Representatives of the Chinese Embassy visited the Iskra Delta showroom. Iskra Delta sales engineers desired to sell as much as possible, so without delay, they prepared an offer for the project regarding the best solution enabling the computer connection of the Chinese police to all major Chinese cities, on the basis of Iskra Delta products and services presented at this event.

Toward the end of the fair, the Chinese came again, this time in a larger number, and requested a demonstration of the offered solutions. When they were satisfied that the Iskra Delta engineers could deal with everything they insisted on in the offer and that it was to be without the U.S. experts' help, they thanked Iskra Delta for the presentation in a friendly manner and were happy; they knew they would not receive such an offer from the Americans.

The systems engineer who led the manufacturing of the project offer for the Chinese knew, of course, that Iskra Delta could not sell DEC products outside of Yugoslavia, but since this was all designed on computers that Iskra Delta sold under its name, he was convinced that the management would receive the appropriate licence, bearing in mind the value of this project was approximately $10 million. This engineer also did not inform the senior management that he had already handed a framework contract with an offer to the representatives of the Chinese government because he did not believe that the Chinese would really accept the offer because of the high price that was stated. The managers, therefore, found out about this project when the contract was already signed.

The Chinese knew that such technology, mastered by Iskra Delta, could not be bought in the U.S. because it was under the U.S. embargo; therefore, this was for them a unique opportunity. They already had the offer in their hands and were aware of the need for further good relations between their countries, as well as the need to engage the Yugoslav government to ensure that Iskra Delta could progress with the offered project. Therefore, the Chinese government, soon after the end of the fair in Zagreb, sent an invitation to the Yugoslav government for the representatives headed by the Interior Minister to visit China and sign an important contract between the two governments on development cooperation between the police forces of China and Yugoslavia.

The Yugoslav government was surprised by the unexpected invitation, but they immediately responded and sent a delegation to China, headed by the Interior Minister and the director of the Institute for the Development of the Belgrade police. The Chinese government welcomed the Yugoslav delegation with full honours, probably so its members would be most cooperative in the proposed cooperation on the basis of the prepared contract for the purchase of the computer network with Vax-compatible computers developed by Yugoslavia and the creation of application programs for the operation of this network, which would be a joint development of the Chinese and Yugoslav engineers.

As the representatives of the Yugoslav government were not aware of previous discussions between the Chinese and the Iskra Delta representatives, they were, therefore, all the more surprised when the Chinese praised the achievements of Yugoslav Iskra Delta and stressed that they wanted to have all the solutions made only with its equipment for the price they had received at the fair, which was clearly stated in the contract. This was then presented to the Yugoslav delegation.

No member of the Yugoslav delegation was a computer expert, so nobody even knew the details of this contract. They did not even know the background of how it occurred, so they were all in amazement until the Chinese explained that they received all the information regarding the contract from Yugoslav Iskra Delta representatives at the fair in Zagreb.

On receipt of the invitation from the Chinese government, the members of the Yugoslav delegation thought it to be a political agreement on principles of cooperation, rather than a concrete project, and did not expect that they would discuss a most demanding technological project in which computers played a key role, establishing and connecting a network with a completely new technology.

When the director of the Yugoslav Institute for Security realized that the whole purchase was from one firm, which at the time and in his opinion was not even valid in Yugoslavia, he protested and wanted to replace part of the Iskra Delta equipment with equipment from EI Niš and Energoinvest from Sarajevo, to meet the requirements of the all-Yugoslav character of the transaction. But he was not aware of the complexity of the project and did not know that the

Chinese could not buy it from the Americans, who were the only ones to manage computer network technology at that time yet never offered it to anyone other than their closest allies and strictly prohibited its export.

The Chinese knew that their expectations could only be met by Iskra Delta due to its close cooperation with the Americans, something they were already convinced of, and requested in the contract that Iskra Delta supply and install all the equipment, but they allowed it to be agreed in Yugoslavia who else would be involved in this project. The Yugoslav Interior Minister, who was from Slovenia and knew Iskra well, but not its new Delta members, irrespective of the fact that he did not inform Iskra Delta of the subject of a precontract, at the insistence of the Chinese and attending to the beginning of good interaction between the two governments, just signed the proposed contract before leaving with the relevant Chinese minister.

In doing so, he also did not know whether the price was appropriate; because of the insistence to sign immediately, he had to believe the Chinese, who argued that the price was determined by Iskra Delta in the offer to their delegation during their visit to Zagreb. This is how both sides, satisfied, signed the first interstate contract, worth more than $10 million. This contract was China's largest acquisition in Yugoslavia at that time and was the first concrete form of cooperation between the two countries. Operational holders for the fulfilment of the contract with full powers were the respective national security institutes in both countries.

After returning from China, the Yugoslav Interior Minister informed his government about the contract he had signed with the Chinese and then presented it as the greatest achievement in cooperation between the two countries. Immediately at its presentation at the government session, some members questioned whether Yugoslavia would be able to meet the contract's conditions and were concerned even more about which Yugoslav companies would get the deal on its basis. When the government learned that the Chinese were able to choose the company for the fulfilment of the contract themselves, choosing Iskra Delta, which had only just begun to assert itself in Yugoslavia, the members of the session requested that the Institute for Security, the holder of the responsibility of the international agreement on the Yugoslav side, do everything in its power to assure that other established Yugoslav companies participated in the deal.

The Interior Minister was aware that it all really depended on Iskra Delta, based in Slovenia, and the members of Iskra and Gorenje, and therefore, he requested that the general director of Gorenje hold an informal meeting with the director of Iskra Delta. As everything had to take place in strict secrecy, the director of Gorenje organized a meeting in an unusual place and the director of Iskra Delta arrived on the pretext of a working visit, not knowing what the purpose of this abnormal and emergency meeting was.

Only upon arrival did he learn that the Yugoslav Interior Minister was going to come to the meeting and that the interview would be about something that was very important for Yugoslavia. The Interior Minister came alone, with a minimal escort and, without the preliminary formalities; with a sharp tone of voice, he started to talk to the director of Iskra Delta. He told him that he had had to sign a contract with the Chinese government and he did not know whether or not it could be met by Yugoslavia because the Chinese had insisted that they wanted to buy the solution Iskra Delta had suggested to them. He threatened him with what to expect if Iskra Delta was not able to successfully complete in the name of Yugoslavia everything he had signed with the Chinese, and then emphasized that he would be personally responsible for the fulfilment of that contract.

As the director of Iskra Delta at that time still did not know what the project was about and what Iskra Delta had to do, he listened to the minister's threat without comment, because, above all, he knew that it would be quite unwise to contradict this man who was then a very powerful figure in the country. When he spoke, he acquainted the minister with the achievements and explained the development strategy; from that point, the talk continued in a more relaxed atmosphere.

At the end of the several-hour-long meeting, the minister was fully informed about the plans and problems of Iskra Delta in its outgoing development for the first time. Given this information and all the good he had already heard about Iskra Delta in China and its intention to deepen the cooperation with Iskra Delta and Yugoslavia, he became visibly more relaxed and happy at the prospect of the signed contract being successfully fulfilled. He pointed out that, by signing this contract, the development of Iskra Delta was also important for the development of Yugoslavia as a whole. Before leaving this unusual, secret meeting, he promised all the necessary support of the Slovenian and Yugoslav police to safeguard the fulfilment of the contract.

The director of Iskra Delta, shortly after this meeting, about which he was not allowed to speak even with his closest colleagues, received a call from the Institute for National Security in Belgrade, formally passed to him by a representative of the Slovenian police force. He was instructed to come at a given date to the Office of the General, the director of the Institute, and was informed that this was an important national project and must adhere to the rules of state secrecy, and, of course, he had to come alone. When he arrived at the Institute on the appointed date, he was kindly welcomed by the director who then made it immediately clear what the Institute meant to Yugoslavia and what power he himself had within the Yugoslav police. The director of Iskra Delta was then given a declaration of state secrecy to sign, since he would thereafter be presented with a document that was among the most stringent state secrets.

After the director of Iskra Delta signed the declaration, he was told that the Interior Minister had signed a contract with the Chinese government for the supply and construction of a computer network for the Chinese police to be carried out by the Institute, and for this they needed the help of Iskra Delta and some other prominent Yugoslav companies. The director of the Institute then handed him an already prepared contract between the Institute and Iskra Delta; this included the configuration of the computer network, which was stated in the contract with the Chinese, as well as all the work to be done which Iskra Delta and the Institute were obligated to fulfil.

For the work to be performed by the Institute, which was primarily logistical in nature, the director of the Institute demanded 5 percent of the contract value. When the director of Iskra Delta examined what work and supplies should be performed by Iskra Delta, he immediately determined that there was enough money for all parties involved, and without hesitation agreed that the Institute should receive the required percentage for its services, but he required at least three days to check if Iskra Delta would be able to obtain through its U.S. partner the American licence for the sale of its Vax processors, which were listed in the configurations of the Iskra Delta computers.

When the director of the Institute learned that Iskra Delta did not produce all the components of the computers in the configuration offered to the Chinese, he was visibly angry and requested that he not discuss this business with anyone because the entire transaction was a state secret, and that he should solve the problem alone in any way possible.

The director of Iskra Delta tried to explain to him that President Tito had already agreed with the Americans that Yugoslav companies, in order to export their products, including U.S. high-tech parts and sub-assemblies, had to previously obtain a proper End Use Certificate, which was already recognized between the U.S. and the Yugoslav government. The director of the Institute said that in this case that would not happen because all the work had to be carried out in strict confidence, and Iskra Delta should therefore meet its obligations without informing the Americans about where and for whom the computers with the Vax processors were intended.

Soon it was crystal clear that the director of Iskra Delta would not sign the contract with the Institute without the relevant American licence, thus the director of the Institute accused him of being an American CIA agent and that he did not want to have anything to do with him anymore. Suddenly the director of the Institute stood up, angry, left the room, and locked it behind him. The director of Iskra Delta was convinced that he had gone to consider the matter in peace and that they would jointly find a way out of this situation. After spending an hour alone without anyone appearing, a uniformed member of the Institute informed him that he could not leave the room until further notice. When he mentioned that he had a plane to catch to Ljubljana within an hour, the Institute employee replied coldly that he would not see Ljubljana on that day. Then he turned and left the room, locking it again behind him.

Only then did the director of Iskra Delta realize that he was in trouble because he had directly refused to sign the contract on the grounds that he needed to obtain permission from the Americans for export to China on the basis of the agreement between the governments regarding the End Use Certificate, and the director of the Institute for Security could not understand that. Since the phone was in the room, he tried to call Iskra Delta and tell them what happened and where he was, but an assistant at the Institute did not want to connect him, saying that he was waiting for instructions from the general, the director of the Institute, regarding what to do with him.

When darkness started to fall, the question became how to spend the night; he began to beat at the door again. The assistant entered and told him that he still had no further instructions, but he promised that he would bring him a sandwich and coffee and order a procurement officer on duty to provide a bed where he could sleep, unless he received new instructions from the general in the meantime. And since no new instructions arrived, he had to spend the night with the sandwich and coffee in an emergency bed, not knowing what would happen to him the next day. All night he wondered how to resolve this situation, since he was only too aware of what would happen if he were to be imprisoned under the charge of being a foreign agent, likely without a trial.

While contemplating the situation, he came to the conclusion that he had to, at any cost, get in touch by telephone with the Minister of Finance, with whom he had already worked, because he knew that if anyone, he was the person to understand the importance of the Yugoslav agreement with the Americans on the export of imported U.S. technology products from Yugoslavia to third world countries. Early in the morning he tried again to make the call. It was answered by the secretary of the general who was, fortunately, already in the office, and enabled him to connect to the Cabinet of the Minister of Finance.

He was relieved when he immediately connected with the Head of the Cabinet for the Ministry of Finance, whom he knew personally. He told her that he needed to speak with the minister urgently and asked her not to put down the phone at any cost and to go and find the minister, wherever he was, because it was an important national issue and that the information he wanted to communicate was also important for the minister and the government.

After a few very painful minutes, the minister answered the call. When he told him where he was and why he was being detained, it was immediately clear that the government should take immediate action to avoid any complications with the Americans because right at that moment he himself was concluding an agreement with them for a new loan to Yugoslavia by the Exim Bank. He assured the director of Iskra Delta that the issue would be raised at a cabinet session later the same morning, as he was just then preparing for the meeting.

The minister later said that once he managed to explain to the members of the government why he insisted on obtaining permission from the Americans, it became clear what negative consequences this would have had for the Yugoslav economy and the whole country if Yugoslavia were to end up on the U.S. government's so-called black list for U.S. exports of advanced technology. Since it was also very important for the government to fulfil the conditions of the international agreement with the Chinese, they adopted a decision at that same meeting to send a state delegation to Washington DC with the mission to obtain the appropriate U.S. government authorization in order to uphold their agreement with the Americans and to solve such problems.

The Minister of Finance was appointed as the leader of this delegation; the other members were the Vice Chairman of the Federal Chamber of Commerce, the ambassador for the military and economic attaché of the Yugoslav government in the U.S. and the director of Iskra Delta. A very important aspect in this was that the Minister of Internal Affairs and other members of the government realized the importance and meaning of the U.S. export licence, and also that the Vice President of the Federal Economic Chamber, who was previously General Manager of Iskra, was aware of the importance and meaning of the U.S. licence, too. From his own experiences, he knew exactly what importing advanced technologies from U.S. companies meant for the development of Yugoslavia, so he turned to the Interior Minister in a letter in which he explained what negative consequences the Yugoslav economy would suffer if they were to export, without U.S. consent, computers to China containing American high-tech components, which were on the embargo list of exports outside of Yugoslavia.

The Federal Economic Chamber normally did the operational work for the licences and also issued End Use Certificates according to the agreement with the Americans. Therefore, the appointment of the Vice President of the Federal Chamber to the national delegation was all the more relevant because the chamber had shown the Americans the importance that the Yugoslavs placed on licences for the export of American technology, which would be present in the Iskra Delta computers for export to China.

Until the government meeting was over, the director of Iskra Delta was waiting, locked inside the room. Around noon, the director of the Institute entered with a friendly demeanour and began to explain that there had been a misunderstanding and that he now finally understood why the government could not just circumvent the Americans for the Chinese. Still, he did not seem to find it worthwhile to apologize, and he was only a bit more collaborative, agreeing to sign the contract for the deal with the Chinese only when the appropriate U.S. export licence was acquired.

The director of Iskra Delta was still glad the ordeal was over and that the signing of this extremely important contract was still on the table. He also managed to discuss the situation with his colleagues and focused on the realistic chances of successful implementation of the project, given that such large and extensive works had never before been performed by Iskra Delta. A myriad of issues related to the project began to appear as he realized how much responsibility he would have to assume on behalf of the company and that the deal would surely raise a number of unforeseeable and unimaginable problems in its course.

The first piece of the problem puzzle was the simple fact that the transaction would take place in distant China, about which they knew very little at Iskra Delta. Additionally, they were not fully aware of the size and development of China. The second was the fact that Iskra Delta did not have adequate facilities available to implement and test such a large and complex computer network, which at first sight represented an insurmountable problem.

There were only two promising aspects at the beginning of the project: the contract price with the Chinese was high enough to cover every part of the vast costs, and second, the fact that if they implemented the project successfully, they would obtain the best possible reference, which would allow unimagined development improvements for Iskra Delta.

The director of the Institute had already stressed at the first meeting that in this deal it could not pass that only one company would be represented from only one of the republics, and insisted that Iskra Delta identify the work that could be given to other companies from other republics. The director of Iskra Delta, therefore, requested that Iskra Delta be given sufficient time to review and consider the entire project and the contractual requirements of the Chinese. Only then could he determine who in Yugoslavia could be included in the project, notwithstanding that, according to the contract with the Institute, the only company capable and responsible enough for the project was Iskra Delta.

The director of the Institute agreed and suggested that the contract was only nominally authorized by both parties' initials, and that all the open questions related to implementation of the contract could only be resolved after obtaining proper authorization from the Americans. The director of Iskra Delta required that the amendments he proposed enter the contract immediately. The director of the Institute agreed, since it was already clear by then that not many companies in the world would be able to deliver what the Chinese were requesting, and the Yugoslavs had agreed to implement the idea. He also realized that the Institute, with its own experts, could not conduct the contract itself without Iskra Delta. The contract was initialled by both directors in the presence of the closest associates of the Institute, who would later participate operatively in the proceedings.

Regardless of the sleepless night, the director of Iskra Delta was pleased with the progress, as all the representatives of the Institute, upon initialling of the contract, stated that they would do their best to help Iskra Delta in order that Yugoslavia comply with the provisions of the contract with the Chinese.

# Chapter 10

# The U.S. Government Policy on the Export of Products in the Field of Information Technology

The American government had already realized by the middle of the last century, through its intelligence services, that emerging and rapidly developing information technology would play a decisive role not only for winning the Cold War, but also for the further development of U.S. leadership in the world. American promotion of the culture of self-initiative in this field throughout the world via specific legislation enabled the U.S. to progress rapidly in all technological areas, especially in information technology. The government paid serious attention to it on the basis of development models by a special agency who had been working in secret for many years on how the world would develop.

These models showed that information technology would be the biggest engine, as well as the basis for the development of other future technologies. Therefore, through appropriate legislation, they promoted new, rapidly evolving information technology companies established by engineers who gained specific knowledge in universities with very strong research and development departments through projects funded by government agencies and the Army. These companies were already forming in the courtyards of universities, especially in California, in the Silicon Valley. The rest of the world did not have a social order that would allow the rapid formation of enterprises and the immediate transfer of knowledge from development into practical applications, so American experts had tremendous potential for development and success. Top experts from all over the world travelled to the U.S. because they did not have similar opportunities in their own countries.

Particularly in countries with centrally planned economies, everything was subordinate to plans set by politicians who could not encourage a sense of self-initiative, which the United States promoted; these countries lagged behind in all areas where technology development was quick. As it happened, the fastest development was in the field of information technology, and was why the U.S. immediately assumed a leading position in this field.

The U.S. government adopted certain provisions in parallel with legislation that allowed for rapid technological development, provisions which prevented the fast growing companies from exporting their technologies without the consent of a special agency in Washington DC.

To this end, the U.S. government classified every country in the world into several categories and determined for each one of them what could be exported there and what could not, including knowledge and information in fields that were identified as strategic. The countries that were U.S. allies and NATO members held a special position and the most liberal attitude toward all forms of exchange.

A U.S. government agency was specifically set up to issue licences and special documents for export and to set the rules for American companies that wanted to export high-tech products. This export documentation included an end-user certificate for an exported product, the so-called End Use Certificate, stating for what purpose and where a product was exported from a U.S. company would be used. This statement of the product's final application was completed and signed by the computer user, but it had to be certified by a relevant government agency of the user's country.

The U.S. government reserved the right to verify compliance with the provisions of the final application, since its inspectors could check with the registered user at any time as to whether the computer was really being used for the purposes stated in the End Use Certificate. All company directors who had U.S. firms abroad, including their authorized representatives, had to be aware of the export rules. It was thus easier to export to politically allied countries for the U.S. companies where, based on quarterly reports, the companies' officials could describe for what purpose the customer would be using the computer.

More complex export processes were necessary for exporting to countries with special trade status with the U.S. government, particularly for the export of high technology products. This status was granted to Yugoslavia after President Tito visited the U.S. and was very pertinent for the country, since it closely resembled the status of the countries included in NATO. On this basis, major American companies started to sell their products and services in Yugoslavia via selected representative companies. The first to take advantage of this option at the end of the sixties was IBM, initially offering only older computers for administrative business use.

The signed agreement between the Yugoslav government and China for technical business cooperation with the purpose of supplying the most modern computer network, installation, and training of the Chinese engineers, found Iskra Delta for the first time in a situation where it had to ask its U.S. partner, DEC, for export authorization from the American government for the supply of Vax processors to be installed in Iskra Delta systems for export to China.

DEC immediately explained to Iskra Delta very clearly that the knowledge its engineers had gained while being educated in their school was intended for use in Yugoslavia and not in countries that were not allies to the U.S. Since this was not stated in the basic agreement between DEC and Iskra Delta, DEC soon required an amendment to the existing contract, requested by the U.S. government, regarding the new regulations for the export of U.S. knowledge. Without signing this addendum, the Delta engineers could no longer attend the DEC school in the U.S.

Relations with DEC became increasingly difficult when Iskra Delta seriously started its own development, and particularly once DEC learned that, through the Yugoslav government, Iskra Delta had acquired a very large contract in China and was working on developing a generic computer compatible with the Vax computer. At that time, the Iskra Delta executives were not aware that DEC was under special surveillance by the American administration on account of the Vax-based computers having been selected for the strategic needs of the U.S. Army. DEC was then the leading and largest manufacturer of minicomputers, and as such, it also set standards in this field. Its computers in no way lagged behind IBM computers in performance; in fact, they were considered superior due to being universal, easier to use, and much cheaper.

These computers were used by universities, institutes, and industry; they were also used for business purposes wherever the buyers wanted to work with interactive terminals. These computers were the first to be used both in setting up complex computer networks and where work in real time was required. They had a particularly important role in the U.S. national computer network security under the control of the U.S. Army via DARPA. Because of the universal data bus, they were very easily interoperable with devices from other manufacturers and therefore an extremely important part of automated production processes in industry and other activities. They were also important because various component pieces made by different manufacturers could be installed for a wide range of uses.

Versatility and modern architecture for those times also allowed the DEC computers to be much cheaper than the prevailing IBM computers, so they became increasingly competitive on the market in areas that had previously been dominated by IBM.

In the early 1980s, DEC was one of the most advanced technology companies in the emerging information industry because its computers had the widest range of applicability on the market. It is also important to note that its computers, especially the PDP-10, began to be widely used at universities and research institutes in the U.S. and later in the developed world, as well. This is why there were many application programs available for them for many different fields of use. This was greatly appreciated by users in lower income brackets due to being the fastest and most cost effective way to get application software to automate their businesses. Especially instrumental in the rapidly growing sales of the DEC computers, however, was that users were able to get assistance from professionals who were trained on these computers at universities.

That is why countries that were not in alliance with the U.S. wanted to get their hands on these computers. Since they were not able to buy directly from DEC because of the U.S. policy on the export of products in the field of information technology, they tried to buy them from users and from dealers without the knowledge of the Americans. Because each user had to sign a declaration on the end use of the computer and knew they could be checked by a representative of DEC or the U.S. embassy at any moment, the path to them was very difficult for countries under the U.S. embargo. A separate issue was the high prices these used computers commanded, because every user knew the consequences awaiting them if they sold it without the consent of the Americans.

Iskra Delta had a unique opportunity stemming from the knowledge it had gained from servicing the DEC computers, to make a computer that was compatible with the DEC computer as the heart of its own computer system. This is why it formed its own development department, to create electronics that would be compatible with the DEC electronics on the level of the processor itself and with the system program equipment, according to the generic principle.

Such an approach to development was unique in the world at the time and quickly yielded practical results, especially as Iskra Delta started replacing more and more of the DEC components in its Delta systems with its own. When DEC became aware of this, it immediately requested that the contract with Iskra Delta be amended in such a way that Delta separated its representative part of cooperation with DEC from its primary organization and that this cooperation be based only on the OEM (Original Equipment Manufacturer) principle.

The Iskra Delta executives did not agree to this request because they were aware what heavy weapons they had in their experts' knowledge and in the management of the market in Yugoslavia. They were not, however, aware that DEC could simply take the Iskra Delta experts and set up a new representative organization with them. With the help of a person from the inner organization of Iskra Delta who was entrusted with relations with DEC, the executives were able to transfer the part representing DEC to another company.

Of course, this was not sufficient to stop the development of Iskra Delta computers' compatibility with DEC ones. Iskra Delta soon began showing these developments and its own solutions, mainly at specialized fairs in Zagreb and Ljubljana. At these fairs, there were always a lot of representatives of countries that were under the U.S. embargo, as this was the easiest way to learn how the new and emerging information technology industry was advancing.

These countries under the U.S. embargo began, through their intelligence representatives, to establish ever more contacts with representatives of Iskra Delta and to show growing interest in buying Delta computer systems and solutions. The fortunate circumstance for Iskra Delta was that the U.S. government had not yet requested the End Use Certificate for all computer components. It is likely that, in the early eighties, they underestimated the possibility that someone could make a computer according to the generic principle with commercially available components and compatibility with the U.S. computers.

Export licences for high-technology products were granted to only a few verified companies; export monitoring was under sharp control and offenders bore heavy consequences.

The strategic importance of technological advantage in winning the Cold War was most recognized in the organization of COCOM (Coordinating Committee for Multilateral Export Controls), which was founded on an American initiative at the beginning of the Cold War in 1947, with a mandate to impose an embargo on exports of strategic and military materials and related technologies from the West to the Eastern Bloc.

Controls on exports played an important role in the prevention and interference of modernization and military industry development in the Soviet Union, particularly from the mid-seventies to the end of the eighties, effectively inhibiting the quality improvement of the Soviets' weapons systems during the most delicate period of the Cold War.

Members of COCOM, in addition to the U.S., were Australia, Belgium, Canada, Denmark, France, Germany, Greece, Italy, Japan, Luxembourg, Holland, Portugal, Spain, Turkey, and the United Kingdom. The associate members with special status were Austria, Finland, Ireland, New Zealand, Sweden, Switzerland, and Yugoslavia. The U.S. Pentagon had the most important role in the control of such exports, and within it was a special department for strategic export control called DTSA (Defense Technology Security Administration), which actively participated in determining U.S. military and defence strategy, and therefore also guided the operations of COCOM.

During the Soviet Union's period of aggressively arming itself, the U.S. chose a wise, long-term strategy. It did not follow the quantitative superiority of its large rival, but instead decided to bet everything on the quality and accuracy of its weapons systems and the structure and systems of NATO. The qualitative superiority of Western weapons was proved in the 1982 military conflict between Syrian and Israeli aircraft in the Bekaa Valley, where the Israeli American F15 and F16 jets easily destroyed the Syrian Soviet MIG 21 aircraft, and before that also destroyed the radar systems of the Syrian air defence. This was an illustrative demonstration in the dominance of American technology over Soviet technology.

With what zeal the U.S. struggled to maintain its technological edge can also be seen in the stringency of controls on the exports of all members of COCOM to the Soviet Union. When in the years 1982 and 1984 the Japanese producer Toshiba sold computer-controlled machines to the Soviet Union without the required export licence, it was sanctioned with the prohibition of the export of its products to the U.S. for a long time. In the meantime, the Soviet Union improved the production of its submarines with the precise Japanese machinery to such an extent that the U.S. had to make additional efforts to improve its submarine detection systems; otherwise, the Soviets would have become far superior in this field.

The Soviet Union was increasingly aware of its technological lag, although it invested all its development capacities into the development of military industry. This lag was most evident in electronics and information technology. To resolve this situation, the Kremlin decided to organize a special directorate within the KGB, known as Directorate T, with the task of trying to get its hands on Western technology by any means possible, whatever the cost. To this end, it organized a network of brokers-agents in the West, who organized fictitious companies that were buying computers and other technological equipment inside the U.S. Thus they avoided the U.S. export licences, and then exported this equipment through other companies to the Eastern countries, primarily to the USSR. The countries through which these agents acted were mainly Austria, Switzerland, Germany, the United Kingdom, Sweden, Holland, Canada, Finland, Denmark, Belgium, and South Africa.

The most important and the most successful exporter of the prohibited American technology to the East was Richard Muller, who was most famous for the illegal export of the DEC VAX-11/780 computers, which had the widest range of applications in the commercial, developmental, and military fields at that time. This computer was very important for the communications sector, as well, particularly as a hub for computer networks, and especially for use in the graphic design of new microcircuits in the production of microprocessors and other devices. The Pentagon was most afraid that the Soviets could use these computers to significantly improve the accuracy and reliability of their missile systems, so they themselves did all they could to disable Muller in time and prevent him from completing the plan for the export of this computer.

In the West, these agents of the directorate were called techno-bandits, for their ruthless aggression in their work, and they were quite successful. The CIA discovered in the early eighties that the Soviets were rapidly reducing the lag in technological development; this was particularly evident in the manufacture of semiconductors. This discovery led to the conclusion that the Soviets would continue to reduce the technological lag if the West did not take stricter measures to control the export of strategic technologies outside the Alliance. Such a tightening of controls at the time was possible because the U.S. government was able to prevent exports from the United States with the relevant legislation and public information. It got COCOM members on its side for enhanced control of who was completely dependent on the U.S. companies in the field of IT technology, and they also bound some other neutral countries and some Non-Aligned countries.

The leading Western countries, especially Great Britain, wanted a milder form of embargo on exports of high-tech products, which also included computers, to the East and therefore tried to resist the American pressure. The United States threatened Great Britain with an embargo on exports of computer components in the years of Prime Minister Margaret Thatcher and President Ronald Reagan, due to Britain's lack of control and failure to comply with COCOM's instructions, regardless of their great friendship. Only after this threat was the British government shocked to realize that the computers manufactured in the UK were totally dependent on U.S. components.

It was probable that, for the British, the horror of their dependence was all the greater because they knew that the first operational electronic digital computer, called COLOSSUS, was made in Great Britain, in Bletchey Park, during the Second World War and placed into operation in 1943 to destroy German communications ciphers. American engineers participated in the making this machine, and acquired the relevant experience which enabled them to become leaders in creating the American computer industry in the post-war period. Large investments by the U.S. government for the progress of computer technology helped the rapid growth of its companies to develop and produce computers that took the lead in the world and irresistibly overtook their British teachers.

Realizing this, the British had to bow to American pressure and start the accelerated implementation of export control according to the COCOM standards.

The result of this was that the Soviet techno-bandits found themselves amid overwhelming complications in their ability to steal Western technology, so the technological gap between the East and the West in the late eighties was again such that the Soviets had no more options left to modernize their weapons systems, even though their total research and development sphere worked only for the military program.

The insurmountable problem to them was the lack of computers and appropriate electronic equipment for the design and manufacture of modern radar and other weapons systems. The technological gap had an even more devastating effect on their overall economic development; there was a lack of consumer goods, and the public frustration increased in all countries of the Warsaw Pact.

It is no wonder that Soviet President Mikhail Gorbachev, visiting French President Mitterrand in 1988, admitted that the Soviet Union was not a modern country. He had neither modern technology nor fast and powerful computers, but only a banana republic with nuclear weapons.

This recognition by Gorbachev was especially noted in the report for the U.S. Senate and the first director of the DTSA, and clearly stressed the value of the strict embargo on the export of strategic technologies for a bloodless victory in the Cold War between the East and the West.

# Chapter 11

# Presentation of the Computer Network Project for the Chinese Police in Washington DC

At the time it acquired the project deal with China, Iskra Delta was completely dependent on imports of Vax processors from the U.S. These processors, and particularly the systems based on them, were under strict U.S. embargo for all countries not in their closest alliance. This was soon understood by the director of Iskra Delta, when a DEC representative responsible for relations with Iskra Delta clearly stated that DEC did not intend to expose itself alone in order to obtain an export licence in Washington DC solely to benefit Iskra Delta's project in China. He was afraid they would have problems with the administration in Washington DC because he had made it possible for them to achieve such development, to the degree that now they had independently offered the latest information technology to the Chinese. He was willing to help, but only if requested by the U.S. administration to provide answers to technical questions and questions about the technological level of Iskra Delta.

Iskra Delta's director, appointed to the Yugoslav delegation to present the Chinese project to the American administration, was well aware that whether Iskra Delta would be authorized to export Vax processors in its systems to China by the U.S. administration depended entirely on this presentation. He was appointed to the delegation primarily to interpret how these systems would be used by the Chinese police and what the original contribution by Iskra Delta to this project would be, as well as that of DEC.

In the short time remaining before the departure of the delegation to Washington, the leaders of Delta development departments discussed the details of the project at specific workshops and informed the director what Iskra Delta could do with non-American cooperators and what they needed to buy in the U.S. In preparing the documentation to obtain the licence in Washington DC, it became obvious that the most critical points within the Delta systems were the Vax processors and system software, without which the completion of the contract with the Chinese would not be possible. Iskra Delta had already started the manufacture of video terminals, other various communication interfaces, cabinets and system power supply units and the Partner personal computers listed in the contract with the Chinese police, which were intended in the project to be used as intelligent terminals. At the OEM market, they purchased, for example, disk units Japan, and printers and tape drives from other U.S. producers who were not under strict embargo. They developed the computer networking software, which was also of great importance for the completion of the project, according to the generic principle based on similar DEC software and sold it under the name Delta Net.

In preparing the presentation documentation, the realization that Iskra Delta did not need the training experts from America to complete the project was important; Delta's experts could themselves adequately educate the required number of Chinese police in the operation and maintenance of the offered computer network experts, without any external assistance. The Iskra Delta experts who intended to participate in the Chinese project, called Project Billion, assumed personal responsibility in the preparation of presentation documents to ensure that everyone did what they undertook to do in preparing the documentation. The director acquainted himself with all the details, as well, especially those related to the development achievements. Thus prepared and equipped with the presentation material, he travelled with the delegation to Washington DC, where, on arrival they were informed by the Yugoslav Ambassador of the location and the programme for the presentation of the project to the U.S. administration.

According to the ambassador's words, a successful demonstration of the project would be the basis on which the request of the Yugoslav government would be considered, so that the Americans would without exception allow the U.S. company DEC to sell to the Yugoslavs the required equipment for the fulfilment of the contract with the Chinese government. The very composition of the delegation headed by the Minister of Finance and Vice President of the Federal Economic Chamber made it clear how crucial the requested permission was for the Yugoslav government. This was evident the next day when the delegation was welcomed by the appropriate Secretary of the U.S. administration, who stressed right from the beginning the importance of good relations between Yugoslavia and the U.S. and went on to say he appreciated the fact that Yugoslavia adhered to the contract with the U.S. government regarding the export of high technology to Yugoslavia. But it was noticeable that he was undoubtedly the most interested in the details of the project in China, especially considering that the United States did not have good relations with this country at the time.

The head of the Yugoslav delegation also pointed out how his government appreciated how quickly the meeting was organized and that he expected a favourable decision on the application. After this initial, polite formality, the delegation was invited to the special hall for the presentation where a big surprise awaited them, as they did not expect involvement from such high-level representatives from the U.S. administration. When the participants began to introduce themselves, the delegates realized that the Americans took this presentation much more seriously than they themselves had expected. There were representatives of all relevant government, intelligence and other agencies, including the

Pentagon, a total of more than thirty people. Also present was a representative of DEC in Washington DC.

The meeting was chaired by the Undersecretary at the U.S. Department of State in charge of Europe. After a brief introduction, the floor was given to the leader of the Yugoslav delegation, who explained in a few words why, in this case, the licence for the export of American technology to Yugoslavia was so important. He then said the project would be presented by the Yugoslav director of Iskra Delta, who would also answer any specific questions.

This was the key part for the successful completion of the project. The director of Iskra Delta started with a presentation of the company and its relations with DEC, stressing that during this cooperation they had all learned a lot. Their positive results on the Yugoslav market each year had resulted in a sharp increase in the growth of sales for DEC computers and services, and the result of this was that, due to the lack of foreign exchange, Iskra Delta was forced to start replacing imported components and services with ones it developed on its own. Otherwise, it could not maintain the rapid growth and development to meet the market's needs.

This was followed by a detailed presentation of the products and services that Iskra Delta had developed on its own. The director also explained that Delta had gained additional production and development opportunities upon joining with Iskra, and thus was in a position to further enhance cooperation with DEC. Since Iskra Delta became its first OEM partner in Yugoslavia, this subsequent period had allowed even further increases in the market share and the volume of transactions with DEC. Following the presentation of relations with DEC and the abilities of Iskra Delta, the delegation could only hear a murmur in the hall and see on the faces of those present the complete surprise at what they had just heard.

During the explanation and description of the project for the Chinese police, designed entirely by Iskra Delta and without the knowledge of DEC, which was particularly emphasized, the audience grew more and more astonished because they could not believe that someone outside the U.S. would be able to connect computers on Chinese territory. Questions came from all sides, so the U.S. Undersecretary requested the DEC representative to speak before the general debate and to clarify whether it was really possible that the Yugoslav firm Iskra Delta had acquired such knowledge. He also asked the director of Iskra Delta to be prepared to answer questions upon the presentation's completion because he had clearly surprised and upset all present with it.

The DEC representative rather reluctantly approached the rostrum, since he was aware that DEC could have problems with the administration due to potential violations of laws on the export of high technology knowledge and, therefore, immediately began to explain that he did not know Iskra Delta well enough, and that its organization in Europe was responsible for the Yugoslav firm. He did not deny that Iskra Delta was one of its best partners in Europe, but added that he nevertheless could not believe it could complete such an extensive project without the help of DEC experts, as it had been explained and described by Iskra Delta's director. He also pointed out that Iskra Delta most certainly received only the basic knowledge necessary for installation, servicing, and sales of its computers, and according to information at DEC, the Iskra Delta experts attended only the standard education program provided to customers of DEC computers.

Many of those present demanded during his speech that he check which education seminars in the U.S. were attended by the Delta experts, because they could not believe they had acquired all the skills to set up a computer network in China by themselves. When the Undersecretary realized that the present DEC representative could not answer most of the questions, he announced that the administration would request a special meeting with those accountable at DEC from the seat in Maynard.

The members of the Yugoslav delegation became confused while these reactions by the Americans took place, and they started to realize that Iskra Delta had encroached on areas they should not have. The hope that they would obtain their permission started to disappear. Meanwhile, the Undersecretary again asked the director of Iskra Delta to speak and asked him to give more detailed answers to the questions if he wanted a positive verdict for the permit to export Vax processors in Delta systems to China.

The questions came pouring down. The Americans were most interested in how Iskra Delta would connect the computers between the big Chinese cities, who would prepare the necessary electronics and write the appropriate communication and application software, and what the education of the Chinese experts would be. Before answering these questions, the director of Iskra Delta initially stressed that it would not do anything not agreed to by the Americans and that was only if they received permission to export their computers based on the Vax processors. He also stressed that he and his colleagues wanted to continue to cooperate with the Americans; therefore, they would take into account any recommendations that could be related to the project in China. This assurance was accepted with visible approval. The following questions were very specific and related mainly to how they thought they would establish effective control over the use of computers on the basis of the Vax processors, so that they would not be used for purposes other than those stated in the End Use Certificate.

When everybody present realized that the director of Iskra Delta was able and willing to answer most questions, they became more cooperative and the tension that dominated after the speech of the DEC representative began to subside. The leader of the Yugoslav delegation also spoke and said that his government would make every effort to ensure that Iskra Delta would take into account the American recommendations in the project. He also said that all present could see for themselves that the Yugoslav government took the contract on technical cooperation with the U.S. government seriously. The delegation was thorough in that capacity because they were aware that without granting the U.S. export licence to DEC, its contract with the Chinese government could not be met, and that certainly would not be good for the relations between any of the countries involved. In particular, he stressed that the delegation would like to receive the answer before the end of their stay in Washington DC, and expressed his willingness to answer any questions and concerns they still might have.

The U.S. Undersecretary replied that the present representatives did not expect that, given the presentation of the director of Iskra Delta, a country such as Yugoslavia, could be technologically advanced enough to be able to tackle a most demanding technology project, and especially in a country like China. He pointed out that the director of Iskra Delta made a very good impression with his professional presentation and willingness to do everything in his power so that he and his colleagues at Iskra Delta would adhere to the recommendations, which the U.S. side would undoubtedly require for the project's implementation if the application for the export of the DEC products through Yugoslavia to China was favourably resolved.

He also said clearly for the first time that the required American technology was under strict embargo, and that up to now, none of their "friendly" countries in the world had been granted permission to export these strategic technologies to third world countries. This was followed by more questions, and then the Undersecretary concluded the meeting and thanked the members of the Yugoslav delegation for the extensive presentation of the project and the application for the export licence. He then invited some of the members of the attending government agencies to join him, and together they left the hall.

The Yugoslav delegation went to the Yugoslav Embassy with mixed feelings. The head of the delegation immediately informed Belgrade that the situation with the licence did not look good. After a short exchange of views with the Yugoslav Ambassador on what else should be done to persuade the

Americans in the event of a negative reply, the director of Iskra Delta, together with the Minister of Finance and the Deputy of the Chamber, left for their hotel.

Late in the afternoon the same day, a representative of the U.S. administration appeared at the hotel reception. He had been present at the presentation and requested an interview with the director of Iskra Delta. They met in the hotel's room for confidential meetings, and immediately upon his arrival the representative told him why they would like to talk to him in private. He explained that the granting of the licence did not look good; however, according to the information acquired from DEC in the meantime, they were prepared to issue a licence for export with certain restrictions, if by ad-hering to such limitations and instructions he, as director of Iskra Delta, signed a special document of personal liability, this would be sent through DEC by the U.S. administration.

He made it clear that they knew that he was the master-mind behind the management of the company and that he, as the director, was the most deserving of the fact that until then, Iskra Delta had respected the U.S. export regulations and had not committed any offences. He also acknowledged that they had grossly underestimated the rapid development of Iskra Delta because they never imagined that in Yugosla-via there could be such an entrepreneurial company, similar to the U.S. companies in Silicon Valley. At the same time, he said that the United States would have to change its strategic views of the world if it was proven that Iskra Delta was re-ally capable of carrying out the project. The simulations the U.S. had been performing for fifteen years on the possible development of new technologies and their implementation, done according to global development, did not show them the possibility that anyone might be able to quickly follow without directly copying their products in this field, which was strategically extremely important for the U.S. He also said that if he was prepared to sign the document, which he pulled out of his pocket as a draft, then the agency which carried out these simulations would invite him to participate with his knowledge and information in the simulations of the development of information technologies in the world.

After the director read the draft document and noted that it was not anything special or restrictive, that it only required increased supervision and guidance over the implementation by the U.S., he immediately said that he was ready to sign the document because it did not deviate from his mandate as the director of Iskra Delta.

The representative of the U.S. administration was clearly satisfied after this statement and affirmed that if he guaranteed it with his personal responsibility for the agreed limits of the permit, the U.S. administration would approve the company DEC to export the Vax processors needed for the project in China. It had been agreed by heads of agencies after his project presentation. He also said that the permit would be issued through official channels and he should therefore remain silent on this issue until the receipt of written notification, which he should receive soon.

He informed him that after the meeting with the Yugoslav delegation, they had a very important meeting where some attending members of the administration argued that Iskra Delta would never be able to connect the computers into a network by themselves, as it was designed and stated in the project, and that it was important to prevent the Chinese from using these computers for other, mainly military, purposes.

The director assured him that he personally believed the Iskra Delta experts' assurances that they would be able to succeed in carrying out the project. At this, the representative only smiled and said that if this was so, then it was evidence that the knowledge held by Iskra Delta was strategically important and would require other measures from the U.S. administration, and that this knowledge must not leave the hands of Iskra Delta and fall into the hands of countries that were not in the U.S. alliance.

# Chapter 12

# Realization of the First Computer Network Project in China for the Police in 1986, Connecting the Eight Largest Chinese Cities

After the receipt of the document that the U.S. government would accept the request of the Yugoslav government to export the DEC products to Iskra Delta for the fulfilment of the project in China, the activities for the realization of the project started to take place rapidly in Yugoslavia in various areas. First, Iskra Delta had to legally and formally regulate relations with the Institute for Security in Belgrade and agree to work in such a way that would allow them the greatest possible autonomy in the implementation, regardless of the fact that the Institute was the holder of the business in the agreement with the Chinese. It was also important to grant the request of the Institute that other companies be involved in the project from different Yugoslav republics because of the national character of the contract. This condition was insisted upon by the representatives of the Institute, although Iskra Delta argued that other companies in Yugoslavia were unable to offer such products, as required by the Chinese in the project.

Eventually, it turned out that some companies in Yugoslavia were interested in obtaining the knowledge at Iskra Delta through this project and also in receiving the expected references if the project were to succeed. Iskra Delta

Signature of the Final Acceptance Protocol with
Chinese Government representatives

yielded to pressure in the end to include more companies
from Yugoslavia, proposing Energoinvest from Bosnia and
Herzegovina, and in particular its Department of Electronic
Communications and Automation, since they had previously agreed to cooperate in the energy field. The Institute
for Security then ordered the development and manufacture
of communications equipment from this department at Energoinvest, which was necessary to modernize the telephone
network for the Chinese police, and would be later employed
in the manufacture of their computer networks.

Because the key people at Energoinvest were not aware of
the complexity of the contract, they proudly accepted, but
then, due to their lack of experience in this field, fell behind schedule with the manufacture. To avoid delays in the
implementation of the entire project, Iskra Delta began its
own development of the missing equipment, which proved
to be prescient, as Energoinvest, with the help of Iskra Delta
engineers, managed to make the ordered communication

equipment on time, in the end, as well as test it before its installation in China, thus contributing significantly to the fulfilment of the contract.

Another important issue in the contract with the Institute for Security was the creation of a working group for logistics, communication, and implementation of financial obligations. This was important because the Institute for Security under the contract with China was an intermediate link between Iskra Delta and the representatives of the Chinese police; this is why the representatives of the Institute were present when the contract negotiations by Iskra Delta with the Chinese took place, to oversee that they settled their financial obligations as it was agreed in the contract between the two governments.

In Ljubljana, the Institute for Security concluded a relevant agreement with the Slovenian Secretariat of Internal Affairs, according to which their leaders helped Iskra Delta provide security and support to the local authorities in addressing the administrative complications that arose from Iskra Delta's needs for new personnel and premises. All employees on the project known as Billion had to sign a commitment saying they were willing to work in conditions of the greatest trade secrecy, as requested by the Institute for Safety. The workers of the Secretariat also had the opportunity to monitor the activities of Iskra Delta in Slovenia in the implementation of the contract through the Institute for Security.

This assistance from the Slovenian Secretariat of Internal Affairs was vital, especially in providing adequate space in Ljubljana. Iskra Delta did not have an adequately large space at that time to fit such a computer installation in one place. Its production and development were scattered in various locations throughout Slovenia, which caused many problems and extra costs. Due to the large amounts of computer equipment and its sensitivity to the environment, the only place suitable in Ljubljana at the time was Cankarjev dom.

With the help of the Slovenian Secretariat for Internal Affairs, Iskra Delta managed to convince those responsible in Slovenia to allow the use of premises at Cankarjev dom for manufacturing the computer network prototype. The director of Iskra Delta found it difficult to convince the director of Cankarjev dom to both allow this and to cancel all activities there for more than two months without the public beginning to wonder what was going on.

Good financial compensation for the use of Cankarjev dom, paid for by Iskra Delta, enabled the director of Cankarjev dom to sign the corresponding contract with Iskra Delta and declare to the public that during the period of closure maintenance work would be carried out at Cankarjev dom , the most important institution of culture in Slovenia. As soon as Iskra Delta secured the use of the premises in

Recognition award for Iskra Delta from China Government

Cankarjev dom, it started bringing in computer and other equipment needed for the project with the Chinese. Even the Delta experts who worked on this project got their working places there for the duration of the project, so Cankarjev dom transformed into a real modern factory for a while, instead of the cultural temple for which it was built.

It turned out that without these facilities, which were then fully air conditioned and energy equipped, among the few in Ljubljana, Iskra Delta would never have been able to make and test all the equipment necessary for the subsequent installation in China. Working conditions in Cankarjev dom were very good and the time available to the Delta experts was short, so they worked all day and night to see that all was done and developed on time. Strong motivation for the employees was the awareness that they were working on a prestigious project of great importance for the recognition of Iskra Delta in the world.

After the successful testing of the equipment intended for installation in various cities in China, the day came when it was necessary to test the operations of the networked computers. This test was only a simulation of the future network; hardly anyone was really aware of the enormous distances between the projected Chinese cities where the computers would be installed and which would be connected via Chinese telephone lines by Iskra Delta's carefully selected experts when they went to China.

To simulate the operation of the network successfully took a lot of innovative solutions because none of Iskra Delta's experts had worked or had any relevant experience with such a vast and complex project before. It was also necessary to make the appropriate user documentation in English for the Chinese engineers to take over and maintain the computer equipment and the network. Once they were satisfied that everything worked properly, the experts selected for the installation in China then disassembled the test computer network again and set up a network of parts intended for installation in some areas for transport to China.

This transport logistics operation was prepared and implemented by representatives of the Institute for Security, together with the Iskra Delta experts, as planned by their colleague in charge of logistics, transportation, and handing over the equipment.

Transportation of the equipment was organized from Ljubljana to Belgrade in special trucks driven at night with a police escort. After arriving at Surčin airport, the Iskra Delta representatives who had monitored the transport and dealt with the complications caused by the signature hand-over documentation managed to officially hand over the equipment to representatives of the Institute for Security, who then stored the equipment until the arrival of the Chinese aircraft.

Soon after the Chinese government had been notified by the Institute for Security that the contracted equipment was ready for handing over, they sent a military transport aircraft to the airport, onto which they loaded the equipment under the supervision of the Delta engineers. It was loaded so that it was classified according to individual cities and prepared for later transportation by special cars to the intended locations for installation. This logistical operation worked thanks to good planning done at Iskra Delta and carried out systematically so that, in China, there were no complications in the delivery of equipment for each site, even though they were thousands of kilometres away.

The contract also provided for an additional extremely important phase: the implementation of training for the Chinese professionals. More than a hundred people went to be trained in Yugoslavia. They all had a basic knowledge of theoretical computer science, obtained in Chinese and foreign universities, and some of them even had doctorates. They were very motivated and eager to start training. On arrival at the Delta school centre, they had with them a list of fields in which they wished to deepen their knowledge.

Most of these requests were related to in-depth knowledge of Vax technology, manufacturing methods of user applications, and in the field of connecting computers to a network or computer communications. In these areas, Iskra Delta had received a maximum limit in the permit for the export of the American Vax processors in its systems to China. So it was necessary to prepare specific school literature and user documentation for the Chinese experts. This took into account all the constraints specified in the licence; however, they were not allowed to use the original DEC literature.

The Chinese were surprised when they came to the Delta training centre in Nova Gorica and found it to be near the border with Italy, and even more surprised by the fact that there were no specific border guards. They were also taken aback by the training centre equipped with modern classrooms and by the main computer centre, which used computers of various capabilities from the production program of Iskra Delta.

The reception at the modern Delta hotel and the professional approach to education also made a good impression on them, as there was a school centre waiting for them, equipped with a video terminal and relevant literature. They could not believe it when they saw that bicycles were also waiting there for them, for excursions in the immediate vicinity. Iskra Delta decided to use the bicycles not only to pleasantly surprise them, but also so that they could unobtrusively organize their free time, since Iskra Delta was responsible from the moment of their arrival at the training centre for their welfare and safety. Certainly it was in Delta's interest that the Chinese experts felt good and came to know as many of its products as possible, since the leaders were well aware that these experts would be very important for the successful operation of the Delta equipment in their own country, and additionally for further sales of their products to the large Chinese market, which had started to open widely for Iskra Delta.

This was especially important when they presented their latest Trident multiprocessor system. The Chinese did not hide their enthusiasm for the design and performance of the system and, in turn, made declarations that they could not believe that this product was fully developed at Iskra Delta and that they needed thousands of them, which representatives of the management of Iskra Delta believed, though they were not fully aware of the size and capabilities of a country like China.

The experts at Iskra Delta were also motivated, so they put a lot of effort into their work with the Chinese. It was the first time they had given lectures for such a large number of foreign experts, and being experts from China was even more interesting because it was a mysterious country at the time. All lectures were mainly held in English, but the Iskra Delta executives had found some experts with knowledge of Chinese; this contributed to an even more genuine relationship and added a personal touch, as was subsequently shown to be a decisive factor in installing a computer network in China where some of the complications were resolved quickly on a friendly basis.

Iskra Delta undertook the computer network installations after careful preparation, both in Yugoslavia and later in China. First, it sent forth experienced experts to assess the thirteen planned locations in the eight major Chinese cities. The premises at the locations were mostly at the regional police headquarters the Chinese had prepared for the installation of the computer equipment under the instructions of Iskra Delta. At that time, many factors were important: how the space was used, whether it had the infrastructure necessary for the normal operation of the computer equipment, giving special attention to establishing a stable electric power system, cleanliness, and the need for a climate controlled room where the computer equipment was to be installed. It turned out that the Chinese had prepared and equipped the premises intended for the equipment installation according to the Iskra Delta instructions very well.

The experts of Iskra Delta even prepared the documentation in advance for their first visit to the planned cities and, accordingly, to the Chinese requirements set out in the bilateral agreement. This consistency paid off later when it was

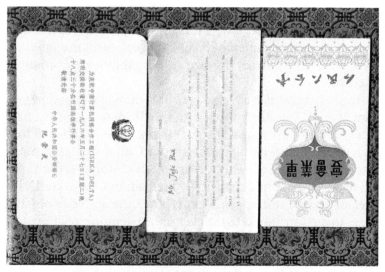

Invitation on banquet from Chinese
minister for Public security

necessary to demonstrate that the computer network was
working as intended in the contract. The duration of the installation and the number of professionals needed for the
installation of equipment and installation of the computer
network had previously been negotiated. Since the locations
were all over China, four in Beijing, and one in each of the cities of Harbin in Manchuria, Xian, Taiyuan, Xiamen, Shanghai,
Shenyang, Tianjing, Wuhan, and Guangzhou in the south, two
installation teams were formed, called North and South.

Each team consisted of Iskra Delta and Chinese experts,
previously trained at the School Centre of Iskra Delta. Following the takeover of equipment in Beijing, the Chinese
side had made no mistake in the chosen transportation to
the final site. To know all the details and potential problems,
the installation project was designed so that the installation
was carried out first on location in Beijing, where the entire
team of Iskra Delta worked and met with the key developers
of the installations on the Chinese side. The project manager

for the installations and setting up the computer network on the Iskra Delta side kept all the responsible Chinese experts up to date on the whole plan of installation until the final transfer of the entire network. The representatives of the Yugoslav Institute for Security, the Yugoslav Ambassador, and the representatives from the Chinese ministries responsible for the project were also familiar with the whole plan.

The distances between cities for which they were planning the agreed equipment installations were unimaginable in terms of the size of Yugoslavia. Just the distance between the cities of Harbin and Guangzhou is about 5000 kilometres, which is huge even by European standards. Therefore, we can say that this was one of the largest computer networks in the world at that time; it was installed in just one month and was also one of the most demanding logistical and organizational operations ever.

It was, therefore, closely monitored by the relevant domestic and foreign intelligence services, who tried to sabotage the project with well concealed actions, but failed due to the vigilance of the installation teams.

The central location of the network was the Police Academy in Beijing, because this was where the development of applications for the entire Chinese police was also envisaged. Every chief of police in each province, along with their experts, welcomed the installation team and were very friendly, and it was obvious that they all knew the importance of the event from the moment they first came into contact with the modern computer technology and its capabilities.

With this entire network of computers, the Chinese could now, for the first time, transfer electronic mail and monitor the population register in real-time, which they had previously been unable to effectively carry out due because their population increases by millions every year. According to their statements, the application which allowed the effective exchange of information between regions and the control of the movements of persons who had committed crimes was particularly important.

The computer network used special telephone lines that had been previously installed, with all the relevant equipment, by the trained professionals of Energoinvest in Sarajevo, partners in this project. This network allowed the transfer of 4800 to 9600 bps at that time, which was then a solid achievement in regard to the distances involved. Before the Chinese representatives responsible for their end signed off on the hand-over of the equipment, every installation team had to test each individual part of the network and then, for the final hand-over, the operations of the entire network between all the places simultaneously in real time.

After the twenty-four hour test of the entire network, they celebrated the official launch of the service, the logistics centre for the spare parts warranty and post guarantee maintenance. The location of the service centre was near the system location called Beijing I, from where it was also possible to control the operation of all the computers in the network and establish alternative communication links in case of failure of any of the telephone lines or modem equipment. The Service Centre team was composed of Chinese engineers previously had extended, in-depth education at Iskra Delta's training centre in Nova Gorica in Slovenia.

When the Yugoslav Ambassador in China, originally from the Republic of Slovenia, learned that the Chinese had started to sign off the acquisition of certain sections of the network, he was so happy that the completion of the project had proceeded as planned that, out of sheer excitement, he invited a few dedicated members of the Iskra Delta installation team to a dinner he had made himself.

He immediately informed the Chinese Minister of Internal Affairs about the first signed hand-over report, then he, in turn, showed the ambassador many previously signed documents intended for new orders from Yugoslavia, if they were convinced that the already purchased equipment had satisfied their customers.

At the festive ceremony for the signing of the final protocol on the completion of all contractual obligations and the hand-over of the operational network, everyone was present who participated in the successful completion of the project.

After the successful completion of the project, Internal Security Minister Ruan Chong Wu invited the participants to a reception where they were thanked for the successful completion of a very complex and thus far the largest project (the biggest operating computer network in China at the time) between the two governments.

At the reception, the speakers further emphasized the flawless completion of the contract, which was signed just a year before by the Chinese and Yugoslav Minister of Internal Affairs.

The Chinese Minister of Internal Affairs also expressed a request to the Yugoslav Ambassador if the specialists from Iskra Delta might further implement appropriate training for senior professors at the Police Academy in Beijing. At the same time, he invited them to present their achievements to the students at the police academy before their departure, so that they would get to know as much as possible about the development and the use of information technology in the world.

The Yugoslav Ambassador, in agreement with the installation team leader, accepted the proposition, and the training and presentation were carried out to mutual satisfaction.[5]

Following this success in China, relations between the two governments strengthened even further, mainly reflected in the fact that other Yugoslav companies began to receive contracts from the Chinese government. To this end, the Yugoslav Economic Exhibition soon opened in Beijing, where Iskra Delta exhibited its latest products and had a series of successful presentations for Chinese businessmen.

---

[5]The Iskra Delta experts at the installation were: Jože Buh as the leader, Viktor Mrak, Janez Strojan, Ibrahim Akšamija, Stjepan Posavec, Franc Škedelj, Tomaž Janež, Vojko Živec, Dare Šimenko, Mirko Lindtner, Čedomir Edi Andruza, Bojan Barlič, Vili Kalamar, and Zvone Petek.

# Chapter 13

# The Visit of the Chinese Premier Zhao Ziyang to Yugoslavia and Slovenia in 1986

After the Iskra Delta experts installed and tested the operation of the first computer network in China and, at the end of May 1986, had signed and exchanged hand-over documents, the representatives of the Chinese government and the police told them at the closing ceremony that this was only the beginning of long-term cooperation with Yugoslavia and its technology companies, primarily centred around Iskra Delta at that time. With this successfully completed project and the first schooling of Chinese experts in Yugoslavia, a sturdy bridge had been built to enhance cooperation between the two countries, but Yugoslavia could not make the most of the offering.

Because the Yugoslav government completed the contractual obligations in the agreed time and strengthened friendly relationships in other areas as well, the Chinese government, soon after the signing of delivery documents with Iskra Delta, awarded the Yugoslav Ambassador in China a high state order.

At that time, Chinese relations with Yugoslavia improved so much that there was also a visit of the Premier of the Chinese government to Yugoslavia in July of that year, less than two months after the hand-over ceremony for the signing of documents on the successful operation of the computer network. At his special request, they included a visit to

Slovenia in the program of his visit to Yugoslavia. The Chinese wanted to visit the factory of Iskra Delta by any means possible, so they could explore the skills and capabilities of the company that had managed to make its first technological breakthrough and successfully complete such a demanding project, something that, at the time, only U.S. companies were capable of managing, though they were not allowed to sell the latest solutions in the field of information technology to China due to the U.S. government embargo.

That was why the Chinese leadership became so interested in learning more about the Yugoslav socialist economic model, which had allowed the development of such options that it could even compete with the technological development of U.S. companies. The Chinese leadership was obviously convinced that in Yugoslavia they had access to alternative technologies that the U.S. refused to sell. At the announcement of the arrival of a strong delegation, headed by the Premier, they stressed that the successful installation of the computer network and the fulfilment of the contract was an important step toward even closer transnational cooperation and opened the door to other companies in former Yugoslavia.

The political leadership in Slovenia, headed by the President of the Presidency, at the reception in honour of the Premier of the Chinese government, was very surprised by the Chinese desire for a more detailed familiarization of the developments of Iskra Delta, because they had just then learned about the successful completion of the important strategic project for China fulfilled by Iskra Delta.

Because this leadership underestimated the achievements of Iskra Delta at that point, in large part due to the influence and impact the American company IBM had on them, they had adapted the visit of the Chinese delegation in such a way that they only presented the tourist attractions on the coast and the Port of Koper and Cankarjev dom in Ljubljana to the delegation. They organized an interview with Slovenian businessmen who were currently or would have liked to sell to China, but the political leadership did not allow a visit to Iskra Delta, which was primarily why the Chinese delegation wanted to visit Yugoslavia.

It turned out that, at the time, they were not aware of the importance the Chinese side gave to the visit to Slovenia because of its technological development. The Slovenian Prime Minister and his colleagues welcomed the Chinese delegation at the formal residence on Brdo near Kranj, where they held official talks and then prepared a gala dinner for the delegation. Also invited to the dinner were the directors of the company Smelt and the airline Adria Airways, which were most interested in the concrete business in China.

The Slovenian Prime Minister also invited the director of Iskra Delta, probably only because of the specific request by the Chinese delegation, who certainly expressed surprise at the official talks as to why the representatives of the Chinese delegation had not previously had the opportunity to speak with representatives of Iskra Delta in order to familiarize themselves with their work and the further development of information technology, which was a field of great importance for the Chinese.

To the Slovenian public, China was regarded mainly as a backward communist country, too far gone to arouse significant interest of Slovenian companies. This is also why the Chinese delegation was welcomed in such a way in Slovenia. During the presentation at the gala dinner, the Chinese, to the surprise of all present, led by their Premier, paid considerable attention to the director of Iskra Delta, of whom they had also received a lot of information from their own experts who had attended Iskra Delta's school in Nova Gorica. The national government was not fully aware of the importance of the achievement of Iskra Delta in China, so per protocol, the director of Iskra Delta sat with the other company directors who were invited, at the end of the banquet table.

It was evident reading between the lines of the welcome toast of the Chinese Premier that they were astonished by the organization of this short visit to Slovenia and that they regretted, because they were not given the chance, not learning more about the company that had successfully completed such an important project in China that had served as a great incentive for further cooperation with Yugoslav companies. Furthermore, the Chinese Premier, who, on this occasion should be known for behaving, at the least, unusually, turned to the director of Iskra Delta and in front of everybody expressed his country's admiration for the achievements of Iskra Delta in China and his regret that the protocol did not include a visit to the company in their program.

By observing such praise by the Chinese Premier, the present members of the Yugoslav side slowly came to understand that the Chinese were, in fact, primarily interested in Iskra Delta and its development and technological achievements, rather than political relations, which the Yugoslav representatives mostly talked about. Following this praise from the Chinese, the Slovenian Prime Minister also spoke some encouraging words about Iskra Delta and its rapid development and about the support they had in Slovenia as the carrier of the computer industry development in the republic. At the same time, he apologized that it was not possible to organize a visit to Iskra Delta, stating that rapid development was responsible for the fact that the company was located in many different locations, and then he handed the floor immediately to the director of Iskra Delta, who briefly introduced the company and its strategy to those present.

Following the presentation, the director of Iskra Delta responded to questions from the members of the Chinese delegation, which were primarily aimed at him. From these questions, it was clear that the delegation with the Premier consisted not only of politicians, but predominately of computer technology specialists and doctors of science who had been trained in the West.

After dinner and the formalities of the final protocol, the majority of the Chinese delegation crowded around the director of Iskra Delta and buried him with their questions. In particular, they were interested in the development achievements of the company and its dependence on U.S. imports for the components of their products. They knew exactly what to ask, and it was soon clear to the director of Iskra Delta that even their translator was also a computer expert, as he asked technical questions himself. While they were talking about the Chinese needs for computers of different capacities and other computer equipment, he felt quite shocked, as they quoted their immediate needs for computers in such quantities that it could not be achieved, according to the capacity of the company at the time, without taking several years, and under the assumption that Iskra Delta worked exclusively for them.

When the reception was over, the protocol announced the departure of the Chinese delegation back to Belgrade, where they would continue their talks with the Yugoslav side; the Chinese Premier then addressed the director of Iskra Delta again and invited him to visit China with his experts as soon as possible. The director of Iskra Delta thanked him for the invitation and promised that he would come to China himself at the first opportunity, for the next stage of business with China. The representatives of the Yugoslav government who accompanied the Chinese delegation were also surprised over the course of the reception because, until that moment, they could not believe what they saw with their own eyes. The Chinese were only interested in everything related to information technology. In this area, not only Yugoslavia, but the entire world, depended largely on the United States at that time.

At the time, none of the Yugoslav companies except Iskra Delta had developed their own computers and software solutions. It turned out that because of the Cold War and the related U.S. embargo on exports of information technology, it was increasingly difficult for any country to follow the Americans in this rapidly developing field. The Chinese planned that, with the help of Iskra Delta achievements, they could pursue the American developments and get vital access to computers that were becoming indispensable in modern weapons systems and other areas that were key to the management and control of the country. This was the main reason the Chinese delegation, on the visit to Slovenia, showed such interest in the development achievements of Iskra Delta and Iskra as a whole. With this understanding, some prominent members of the Yugoslav entourage aggressively envied the director of Iskra Delta for the interest the Chinese delegation had shown in his company and vowed with bitterness that the Yugoslav government would start to see Iskra Delta and its development with different eyes.

# Chapter 14

## The Role of the Intelligence Services of the United States, USSR, China, India, and Yugoslavia in the Cold War and During the Battle for the Acquisition and Protection of Information in the Field of Information Technologies; Alan Turing, the First Casualty

The Cold War is the term used for the open but rarely direct confrontation between the U.S. and USSR and their allies, which developed after the Second World War. This was not a direct armed conflict between major powers, but the biggest race for conventional and nuclear arms in history, with a focus on technological conflict. The main agents were the intelligence services and their spy operations. In addition to actual, mutual killing of intelligence agents, the race for supremacy was led mainly through atomic armaments.

The main feature of these conflicts was the arms race between the Warsaw Pact and NATO. These clashes primarily took place in the fields of technology and the military, resulting in many scientific discoveries. Particularly revolutionary were discoveries in the field of nuclear and conventional missile arms, which then led to a race to conquer space. Most rockets used at that time to send people and satellites into space were originally developed for military purposes.

Other areas of the arms race were involved; among other things were various missile and anti-missile systems for combat aircraft and nuclear submarines as well as all the corresponding anti-weapons, electronic espionage, and spy satellites. All these areas of the arms race called for major technological and productive investments, which crippled both the main competitors, particularly the Soviet Union. The West played the leading role in all areas, except in missile and space planning, thanks to their leadership mainly in the field of information technology.

The battle for supremacy in this field was cruel. Both sides resorted to sabotage and espionage for the production or prevention of the flow of information necessary for the development of computers and accompanying equipment. The Soviet military leaders and their scientists realized the importance of high-speed digital computers too late, and they reacted only after the West, especially the U.S., had already equipped laboratories and university departments.

The Americans received the initial experience in the manufacture of electronic digital computers from the British, who were leaders in this field at the end of the forties. It is understandable that the founders of most computer companies in the U.S. during the fifties were experts that had previously participated in the development and construction of computers in the UK.

The most successful among them were Howard Engstrom-Norris, who first founded ERA (Engineering Research Associates) and then CDC (Control Data Corporation), a very important company for the manufacture of super fast computers. He also served as the deputy director of the NSA. The other was Ralph Palmer, the technical architect of the IBM transition to electronic digital computers. Because of its cooperation, IBM shortly thereafter became a leading manufacturer of computers for the U.S. Army and administration.

The main sponsor of the newly founded companies working in the U.S. on developing and building the most powerful computers mainly for intelligence services and for the Agency for Atomic Research was the NSA (National Security Agency).

Leading experts in companies, institutes, and universities that participated in IT projects were under its special control, were not allowed to move freely, and were subjected to special surveillance when they travelled to another country.

The first victim in the battle for information technology was the leading scientist of his time in this area, Alan Mathison Turing, who was born on June 23, 1912, in London and died on June 7, 1954, in Cheshire. The official explanation was that he was poisoned when he bit into an apple containing the toxin cyanide.

One of the leading U.S. manufacturers of computers today, the Apple company, perhaps selected its bitten apple logo in recognition of this event.

Turing was a mathematician, logician, and cryptanalyst. During World War II, he worked for the British government and was honoured for the fact that the British-American partnership, using his code breaking skills, defeated the Germans in their battle against the German Navy submarines. Later, he was involved in the allies' programs in manufacturing new coding systems and producing the first practical computational machinery used for the development of new secret weapons.

After the Second World War, Turing was monitored by U.S. and British intelligence services due to his importance, and because he loved freedom more than money and titles, they took painstaking care that he did not come into contact with the Eastern agents because, having been included as a mathematician and inventor in the deepest military secrets, he knew most of them.

Turing first described a program as a set of instructions and created algorithms for the computation of his Turing machine. His contribution is considered to be the beginning of computer science, and advancing his ideas is the basis of to-day's modern computers and artificial intelligence programs.

The American mathematician of Hungarian origin, John von Neumann, who was involved in the American project of producing the first atomic bomb, was well aware of Turing's work, as he invited him, in 1930, to Princeton University, where Turing was instrumental in drawing up the plan for the first multi-purpose research computer for complex calculations in military projects.

Von Neumann ordered the use of computers in physics calculations that were necessary in the execution of the first atomic bomb explosion.

To this end, the United States built ENIAC (Electronic Numerical Integrator and Computer) in 1945 at the University of Pennsylvania, which was used for the complex calculations required in designing hydrogen bombs. ENIAC also significantly contributed to the increased accuracy of the U.S. air defence weapons.

With the detonation of the first Soviet nuclear bomb on August 8, 1953, the Cold War between the East and West intensified, and the possession of computers became even more important, as the British and Americans were increasingly aware of the importance of computers in the research and application of the latest weapons.

Unpredictable and liberal Turing was thus becoming more and more dangerous, as he did not want to be subordinated by military command and even felt that he had the right to transfer his knowledge about his discoveries to friends he had met in the East during the Second World War.

Today it is increasingly clear that his sudden and mysterious death was not merely a coincidence, but a deliberate act by U.S. and British intelligence services, for which a dead Turing was at that point more useful than a live one. They prevented the Soviet Union from coming into timely possession of computer facilities and, consequently, the atomic bomb, which was increasingly necessary in the demanding military research and the applications of new weapons.

Already, between 1940 and 1960, the U.S. military was the most important catalyst for the development of computer technology. If they had not had a clear vision of what role computers would play in their military strategy, computer technology would not be nearly as developed as it is today nor in such common use. Computers played an important role in the U.S. national defence during the Cold War, even before the emergence of the Internet, and there are several examples of how they were integrated into that defence structure.

The first signs of the development of computer technology for the U.S. Army were in its defence strategy in the field of ballistic missile and anti-aircraft weapons. In particular, ballistic missiles were the greatest threat to the U.S. in the notion of an upcoming atomic war which embodied the Cold War.

The Americans had had a bad experience during the Second World War with their anti-aircraft weapons due to their inaccuracy, as those weapons did not follow the development of military aviation in relation to speed and great manoeuvrability. The Americans were aware that this part of their national defence had to be improved. The problem in the Second World War was the need for fast and accurate computation of coordinates, so it was necessary to develop systems for fast computation, which was largely what led to the development of digital computers. The U.S. government allocated funding for several projects at universities and institutes at the national level in order to promote research in the field of computer science.

In this respect, the Cold War provided the initiative for the rapid development of computers that had an immediate and significant impact on the increase in U.S. defence capabilities. During the Cold War, computers played an important role in calculating the exact coordinates for a projectile or ballistic missiles. At MIT (Massachusetts Institute of Technology), a special BRL (Ballistic Research Laboratory) was built for this purpose, which served as a very important step for computer development and use in the Cold War.

Fear of atomic attack had a major impact on accelerating investments in the development of new technologies, and progress in the development of digital computers enabled the U.S. to have an advantage in the use of intercontinental ballistic missiles. The real acceleration in the development and use of computers was caused by the news that the Soviet Union was able to test a nuclear bomb. When the Americans learned that the Soviet Union had nuclear weapons, they immediately prepared a project for an air defence system called SAGE (Semi-Automatic Ground Environment). This project, developed by MIT, was one of the major computer projects spurred by the Cold War.

IBM received the contract for the manufacture of computers for this project from the Department of Defence. It had to prepare them based on the plans and technology developed at MIT. These were the first digital computers to work in real-time, which had, among other innovations, an integrated video display, magnetic memory, analogue-digital and digital-analogue converters, and digital data transmission over telephone lines.

IBM developed fifty-six computers for Project SAGE, each of which cost nearly a million dollars. With their manufacture, IBM also had the latest technology solutions quite cheaply, which helped significantly in further development.

The SAGE project consisted of bases in twenty-three centres around the U.S. and one in Canada, which housed computers for management and airspace control. This computerized communication system was linked with a radar system via telephone lines to protect against low-flying airplanes. These SAGE centres were able to simultaneously track hundreds of planes, with easy communication between computer centres. At that time, the SAGE project was the most extensive and demanding computer project, enabling communication at a national level and effective control of all U.S. air space during the Cold War, and thus a great advantage over its opponents. Shortly after the completion of the SAGE project in the early sixties, the U.S. Department of

Defence started thinking about how to establish an adequate and uninterrupted communications system in the event of nuclear war.

None of the existing communication systems based on central operation were considered in the selection because of the danger of the main communications centre being disabled by a nuclear shock, so it was necessary to build a decentralized network. An appropriate solution was proposed by the RAND Corporation, based on a system of nodes. Each node was the same and each capable of packaging and sending information. The more nodes in the system, the more reliable the system was; even if some were destroyed, others were still operational, storing and forwarding information.

With this developmental thinking during the Cold War, the concept was born on which the Internet was built.

This project was published in 1969 as ARPANET (Advanced Research Projects Agency Network). Upon publication, it had four nodes. Today's internet has a few million nodes worldwide. From the moment it came into use, it became an integral part of the world's development, regardless of it being designed and built during Cold War only to defend the U.S. against attack by nuclear missiles. It enhanced the country's preparedness for nuclear war, since it provided uninterrupted communication throughout the American territory and, therefore, the coordination of the full defence potential available at that time.

Such progress in information technologies impacted the U.S. military forces to the degree that it would fundamentally alter the doctrine of air/land battle warfare if there were to be a conflict during the Cold War. In this revised doctrine, a major role was played by computer communications between weapons and systems that incorporate microprocessors and the latest video communication and sensor systems.

After the end of the Cold War in the early nineties, the use of the Internet gradually spread throughout the world, later serving commercial purposes as well, through institutes and universities involved in its development.

At CERN in Switzerland, Tim Berners-Lee made an important contribution to this development in 1991 by identifying the problem of the constant change of information flow. To solve this problem, he proposed a hypertext system instead of the hierarchical organization or organization by keywords.

Lee's solution operated over the Internet on different operating systems, thereby also providing a foundation for the World Wide Web and the first Web search engine.

From this network, the Internet's growth has exploded to become part of the world's cultural life. Now, in the twenty-first century, the Internet, the child of the Cold War, represents one of the main driving forces of development.

In the Soviet Union, the pace of development of information technology was incomparably slower, and in September 1950, the director of the Moscow Institute of Precision Mechanics and Computer Technology said, at the seminar of Soviet scientists, that their computer science was behind the U.S. by fifteen years. Then he showed some pictures of computers built in the West. He announced that, due to political interests, the Soviet Union had to catch up on the evolution of computers in the West within five years.

An institute was entrusted with this task and was led by a man of exceptional ability, the genius Sergei Lebedjev, who, in the East, was known as the Soviet Alan Turing.

Because of the blockade on information technology from the West, Lebedjev, along with his colleagues, progressed slowly, but their computers could not be compared to the U.S. ones in either capacity or speed. Only in 1958 did he succeed in developing a computer that could go into production. It was called BESM-2, and by 1962 there were around 150 made for the relevant institutions in the Soviet Union, and one was exported to China. The BESM-2 was a 39-bit computer with a commemorative 39-bit bus. It had a ferrite memory of 2 KB with an access speed of 10 milliseconds. The processor speed was 10,000 instructions per second, which was very slow by Western standards.

Around 1960, the Soviet Army began to use computers as an aid in planning, in logistics, and in simulations of military conflict, so it put in a request for more powerful computers. For this purpose, the BESM-6 was built in 1967 and went into full production a year later; this was the first Soviet super-computer. This computer was able in its best configuration to process one million instructions per second, it had 192 KB of ferrite memory, a magnetic disk, magnetic tape memory, input devices were punch cards, paper tape, and even some video terminals. The capacity to process fourteen instructions in parallel at any one time gave this 10MHz computer its supercomputing status. It was invented by Lebedjev, but most technology solutions were still not of Soviet origin, but acquired from IBM.

Although Lebedjev died in 1974, the last BESM-6 was manufactured in 1987, to give a total of 355 computers. By order of the Soviet leadership at that time, they copied everything that IBM did, so in 1968, they began the project of cloning their System 360, with the help of the Soviet KGB. The IBM PC had long been in wide use in the West for various applications, and this was why the KGB chose it for copying. The design for the Soviet version of this machine basically came from the Moscow scientific development centre for electronic computing machines, but the plans and even parts of the hardware were smuggled by the KGB agents from the West.

The Soviet Union could not buy an IBM 360 system lawfully in the West due to the information technology embargo adopted by COCOM.

Notwithstanding such an embargo, the Soviet Union still managed to make more than 15,000 clones of the IBM System 360 by the end of 1994; it was named ES EVM and was used for various applications in science and industry. Since it was based on the initial version of the 360, this computer was not as fast as later versions of this system in the West, but it worked in the Russian language on the OS/360 operating system, which was called OS EC by the Russians.

In 1975, the Soviet Union began to manufacture a clone of the PDP-11/40 minicomputer from the company DEC on the basis of its success with the ES EVM. This computer, called SM-4 EVM by the Russians, had 128KB or 256KB of RAM memory, two 2.5MB flexible disks, two 5MB fixed disks, two magnetic tape drives, a paper tape drive, and a large number of video terminals. This Russian SM-4 imitated the American original PDP-11/40 so well that it even supported the UNIX software.

In the mid-eighties, the Soviets managed to copy the early version of the IBM PC, which they called ES-PEVM. It supported early version of DOS and Windows. It was developed in Russia and produced in Minsk in the organization for the manufacture of computing machines. The American intelligence agencies not only watched these developments, but also closely supervised the copying of the Western computer technology at all times.

A ground-breaking event took place in 1981 at a meeting between U.S. President Ronald Reagan and French President Mitterrand, when Mitterand informed the U.S. president that the French intelligence service had gotten a KGB agent in Moscow to their side, an agent known as Farewell. This agent was responsible for the evaluation of Western computer technology and had access to the KGB leadership department that was responsible for obtaining and copying Western technology developments.

Since 1981, the French intelligence service had helped the U.S. with essential information about KGB operations regarding the stealing of Western technology. The most important information was acquired by Agent Farewell, and they were able to determine in the West precisely how and by what means the KGB had access to Western technology data. Through him, they discovered most of the KGB agents in the West who were responsible for the acquisition of technological information. Crucial for the West was information on the agent's list, in which the major technological needs in the field of information technology were stated, developments the Soviet agents very much wanted to obtain in the West.

Based on this information, the president of the U.S. asked the CIA director how to best take advantage of the agent's information. After careful consideration, the agency created and adopted a plan to allow the KGB agents to acquire the desired technologies, but only after they were appropriately defectively modified. This was done so that, for example, they allowed the KGB agents to steal certain microprocessors that passed quality tests but had a special built-in time failure, which was launched after a month, or after one or even several years.

During the Cold War, the idea of planting viruses in software was also born. Their role was to disrupt the proper functioning of the computers after a time, and they performed it more than successfully. Stolen modified technologies suddenly started to cause major damage to the Soviets, and in particular, they further hampered their efforts to catch up with the West in the field of computer technology.

However, between 1984 and 1985, a large number of suspected KGB agents were arrested in the U.S., agents who had carried technological information from the West to the Soviet Union up until then. Consequently, the development and manufacture of computers in the Soviet Union slowed even further, and then drastically eroded. Overnight they no longer knew what was really happening in American development laboratories, as even that which they did managed to steal did not function after a period of time. This was causing so much uncertainty that the KGB agents searched, in panic, for a solution out of this situation.

The solution was found in the non-aligned Yugoslavia, at Iskra Delta. For the socialist environment, this was an abnormally fast growing company, which at that time had already completed the very successful project in China and demonstrated that it had mastered modern information technology and all the necessary skills and technological capabilities it could only get from the U.S. Recognizing that this particular

Yugoslav company was a solution to compensate for the under-development in the field of computers in the East, the KGB grabbed this opportunity and, with all its might, tried to gain access to technologies and products produced by Iskra Delta. This, however, did not go unnoticed by the CIA agents. It led to the situation where Iskra Delta stood in the crossfire of the two world powers at the end of 1986, without being aware of it. Effects were soon felt in its further development, which due to this situation, suddenly became significantly more difficult.

In the East, they realized that the West had triumphed in the most important field of information technologies. In the West, the increased economic benefits from the use of modern computers was reflected in its economy and administration, and it was particularly reflected in the military hardware race because the West, due to better computers, could manufacture more accurate weapons and systems while the East had to use more brute force due to its weaker computers. This was compensated for by inefficiently increasing the abundance of its weapons, which led to significant depletion of resources in the Soviet Union and its allies.

An important feature of the nuclear game was the fear of attacks; both sides knew they had so many weapons that they could destroy each other and the whole world, in the event of an attack by any party there would be no winner. For exactly this reason, direct military conflict between the parties was excluded, and the main role was being played by intelligence services. The largest parts were played by the CIA (USA), MI6 (United Kingdom), BND (West Germany), STASI (East Germany), and the KGB (Soviet Union).

These departments were leading battles in different areas that were important for one side or the other. They had available to them all the state resources needed to achieve their goals. In doing so, they used people on the opposite side, bought to obstruct technological development and to obtain information that would help give them the advantages over the opposing side.

Intelligence services started to lead particularly wrathful battles when the Eastern side discovered in the early eighties that the rapid development of information technology would significantly turn the tide of the conflict to the advantage of the West because the East had not given enough attention and importance to the field of information technology in time. The West, led by the United States, dictated the development during the Cold War and led with great advantage in the development and manufacture of computers for both military and civilian purposes.

More and more computers and products were built in the American automated manufacturing facilities from one day to the next, especially in the latest field of strategic arms, and the U.S. soon became well aware of its technological advantages. Using information gained from spies who worked in the East, they found that the Soviet Union with its allies, notably the East Germans and the Chinese, would not be able to make up these advantages if the Eastern intelligence services were not able to gain the necessary technological information from the West and then form a way to reduce the lag, which heavily influenced the overall development of the economy, especially the defence industry in the Eastern countries. The government of the United States, in order to retain this advantage, prohibited the export of information technologies with an even stricter embargo to all countries not in its close alliance.

U.S. intelligence agencies devoted a special method to monitoring the embargo and the protection of information in this field, so they produced a special guide for U.S. firms that intended to sell this technology outside the U.S. These instructions had to be strictly adhered to by American companies; it was punishable by law with heavy fines if it was proved that any of these companies or their management were exporting to a non-allied country without the permission of the U.S. government. The CIA organized a special DS & T directorate (Directorate for Science and Technology), which primarily employed leading experts from institutes and universities who worked for the directorate on contract. In this way, they ensured mobility of staff, while at the same time, these professionals were also under special surveillance.

The Iskra Delta executives at that time were not sufficiently aware of the importance that information technology was playing in the Cold War; therefore, they did not know what battles were taking place over it between the various intelligence services of the East and West, which would have devastating consequences for the continued existence of Iskra Delta. Easterners realized only at the end of the eighties that Western intelligence services masterfully misled their intelligence services by being able to plant defective components, illegally purchased in the West, to create their own copies of IBM and DEC computers. They also found out that the Americans could disable the computers made in the East through their satellites at any time, which caused genuine panic and put even more pressure on Iskra Delta. This led them to seeing Iskra Delta as the only solution to escape from their problems.

Each side had its own plans with Iskra Delta. To the East, it represented the possibility to genuinely obtain the latest information technology, and for the West, the danger that its technology could fall uncontrollably into the possession of the East, which could have a giant impact on the course of the Cold War between the two opposing sides. This was certainly made apparent immediately after the visit to Yugoslavia by the Soviet delegation headed by President Gorbachev in early 1988, when Iskra Delta suddenly started having inexplicable major financial and domestic problems within a few months of the visit. Such trouble was caused by well organized and carefully concealed pressures from abroad, from both the East and the West.

For fear of development achievements coming uncontrollably into the hands of the Soviet Union and its allies, Western intelligence services applied very strong pressure on the leadership of Iskra Delta to abandon its own development, claiming that it was not worth it and that they should rely on one of the U.S. firms as its manufacturing partner. The pressure felt in the Slovenian government via the Iskra management and some individuals was especially strong, since they also involved journalists and selected individual experts who were creating an impression for the public through the media that Iskra Delta was in financial trouble due to its insistence on senseless self-development. Iskra Delta management always respected agreements with the Americans regarding the export of its computers to the East, so it did not want, without the consent and knowledge of the U.S. administration, to accept offers from the East to transfer part of its production of computers to them for big money and advantage on its market without the knowledge of the Americans.

Since Iskra Delta executives insisted on respecting the agreement it had with the Americans, the Easterners began to blackmail Iskra Delta by retaining payments for already supplied computers, because they knew that it urgently needed money if it wanted to keep up with the scope and pace of its development. They also knew that Iskra Delta would not get the missing money easily, but if it did eventually get it, it would incur very high costs, given the high inflation which was then crippling Yugoslavia. Through their agents, they were also informed that Iskra Delta had no genuine and sincere support of the Slovenian government because of the influence of competing foreign agents on some of its members.

Iskra Delta, therefore, found itself in the middle of the Cold War in mid-1989, in the strong, unbearable grip between the two sides, left entirely on its own, since even KOS no longer stood by its side, due to its own interests and the chaotic situations prevailing at that time between the republics of Yugoslavia.

Because of the intolerable situation of being in the crossfire between the two sides and without the support of the leaders of its own country, the leadership of Iskra Delta discovered that it would not be able to endure the pressure for much longer; therefore, prompted by the director, the members chose to resign from their positions rather than submit to one or the other side of the pressures. This unexpected and sudden move by the leadership astonished all the players, since no one expected the leadership to react in this way.

But the opponents of self-development of information technology in Yugoslavia and Slovenia skilfully used the opportunity and immediately took measures so that Iskra Delta, lacking leadership, came under the expedited procedure and was illegally liquidated as the increasing chaos in Yugoslavia ultimately spread throughout the country.

# Chapter 15

## Intelligence Services in the Battle for Iskra Delta's Information Technology— Inclusion of KOS, the Counterintelligence Service of Yugoslavia

By the end of 1986, Iskra Delta had already mastered an important segment of information technology using its previous projects' approaches and its own development. The company had its own development production program and had been only minimally dependent on the American company DEC since starting its own activity with the American company. This program was composed of several developmental information technology projects:

> PAKA—This was a multi-purpose terminal, the most numerous product and a medium for users to communicate with computers. It was fully mastered in the regular production with Iskra Delta's own perspective of further development and had a huge sales potential to Western and Eastern markets. Special versions of these terminals were also designed, such as a banking terminal and a *point of sale* terminal for use in shops and in many other areas.
>
> PARTNER—This was a classic PC, composed of an integrated processing unit and monitor and keyboard.

Its operating system was CPM, for which there were many applications on the world market, such as a text editor (WordStar), Lotus 123, etc. As a multi-purpose personal computer, it was the most widely used Iskra Delta microcomputer system. As a single-purpose personal computer, it was designed for different types of uses: production, commerce, medicine, and even as an intelligent terminal for the simulation of operating with different types of computers, like IBM, UNIVAC, and CDC. Partner was also used as a small business data processing system in small companies. With it, Iskra Delta learned series production of more complex assemblies and complete computer systems, and produced tens of thousands of units. They were used in various applications, from industry, tourism, trade, banking, etc. Partner was also a strong product for export, particularly to the Eastern market. There were even talks of technology sale for production in the Soviet Union.

LAN (Local Area Network) –This was developed by Iskra Delta Partner for microcomputers based on the operating system CP/M, allowing a transparent way of working for individuals and networks on the same computer. Network properties were completely transparent to all applications and system programs, which enabled the distributed processing of data without additional programming and opened new fields of simple communication between user and computer. The essence of the network was that, through the Partner computer and network, a user had access to the data on all other computers connected to the network, which in 1985, represented an interesting solution and usefulness on the market.

TRIGLAV (Trident)—This was a 16/32-bit family of computer systems for more demanding universal needs. The architecture was based on the VME bus (VersaModule Eurocard bus), which was the global standard, and was intended to be a technological breakthrough with its design and ability to compete in the demanding Western market. The Triglav family represented one of the greatest achievements in the development of Iskra Delta. This family of computers was conceived as a universal computer configurable for different uses and also for sale in parts to manufacturers of machinery and equipment, such as numerically controlled machines, robots, and for process control in industry. Triglav and its parts were especially suited, with its modern design and modern electronics, for the markets of Western Europe and the U.S. At the very beginning of production, hundreds of sub-assemblies and complete systems were sold and delivered to various markets, including the development department of the Mercedes factory in Germany. Quality control of these systems was carried out before delivery to customers at the Iskra Delta factory in Austria. Particularly attractive for the market was the 32 bit computer system Triglav version because it was one of the few multi-purpose super minicomputers at that time and therefore belonged among the leading products in the world in this field. This was confirmed by the gold medal it obtained at the International Fair in Leipzig, Germany. There, Triglav was recognized as the best computer in an open competition of many products from the West, East, and Far East.

DELTA 800 systems—These were developed on the basis of the generic principle-based PDP-11 computer of the DEC company. Production was completely mastered with configurations for different types of uses. This computer was designed for process and business data processing. On the market, it covered the field where the PDP-11 from DEC had hitherto prevailed. Iskra Delta was successful in the marketplace with this mini system primarily in the field of complex process controls and production management with needs for e-mail and video texts as a communication hub. In the export area, this system was designed primarily for the Eastern market as a moderately powerful computer with many applicative solutions already developed.

DELTA 8000 system—This was developed based on the generic principle of the very popular Vax processor from DEC. At the beginning of production, this system required several imported components, but these were gradually replaced with Iskra Delta's own developed and manufactured electronic assemblies and sub-assemblies. By developing its own wiring to the system bus, Iskra Delta managed to produce the most powerful 32-bit computer at that time, and greatly reduce the need for imported components. This achievement in 1988 was important in increasing the regular production of powerful computer systems needed to manage complex production processes and to provide banking and other applications in different sectors of the economy. With these achievements in that year, Iskra Delta became quite independent from the U.S. company DEC but strategically retained its compatibility with this family of Vax computer systems, which were scattered throughout the world. Mastering the production of the Delta 8000 system allowed Iskra Delta further significant development opportunities and the ability to meet the needs of an important market segment for workstations and the automation industry, especially on the basis of CAD/CAM systems.

GEMINI system—This system represented a milestone in the construction of Iskra Delta's multiprocessor 32-bit systems. This system included in the Iskra Delta development the highly developed knowledge and experience in building parallel systems. It was the most powerful and most expensive product of Iskra Delta, intended for complex, demanding data processing.

IDA (Iskra Delta Architecture) – This was software for databases. It led Iskra Delta to independence in a very complicated area of system software and represented one of the most significant achievements in its own development, allowing further self-built, complex computer processing and the construction of information systems for different types of treatment. It was designed to allow distributed processing and databases on different systems within a single information system.

COMMUNICATIONS project—This was developed with its own respective hardware and software for the manufacture of computer networks for the purposes of electronic mail and video text. It was based on the global OSI (Open Systems Interconnection) standards and represented a solid infrastructure on which to build modern computer communications with a strong emphasis on e-mail and video text. This knowledge was very useful to Iskra Delta in the implementation of the Winter Universiade in Czechoslovakia, where it demonstrated distributed data processing time with updated information for television transmissions to different countries for major sporting events for the first time, one of the few such solutions in the world.

DIPS 85—This was a project of process modules of hardware and software for managing processes in real time in industry and the energy sector. As part of this project, Iskra Delta produced computer and sub-assemblies that allowed automation by producers and end users of industrial and domestic power drives. The Army was interested in this project and would use it for monitoring and managing complex weapons systems.

APPLIED BRANCHES project—Iskra Delta, in conjunction with companies in industry, tourism, transport, construction and trade, which were at the forefront of technology control in their fields of work, developed and offered turnkey solutions on the market for the needs of users from these fields.

American intelligence agencies realized shortly after the initial success of Iskra Delta outside Yugoslavia that Iskra Delta was the one company that, in cooperating with the U.S. companies, had acquired critical knowledge and technologies due to the self-initiated policy of its management, oriented toward self-development. If the knowledge and technologies reached Eastern intelligence services, they would be able to catch up with the West and could, according to the U.S. administration, exacerbate and prolong the Cold War between the two opposing blocs. The development orientation and achievements of Iskra Delta were something that they had become acquainted with through Iskra Delta's presentation as part of the request to the U.S. government for permission to export DEC's Vax systems in the Delta processors to China and then later with the incredibly successful and quick installation of then the most extensive computer network between eight major cities in China. That the problem of Iskra Delta was even larger than the U.S. intelligence services had imagined was shown at the presentation of its PARSYS research project to the leading experts of the universities and institutes in the U.S.

Strategic assessment by U.S. intelligence services clearly showed that the U.S. had to take all feasible measures to prevent the development achievements of Iskra Delta from falling into the possession of the Eastern Bloc. U.S. actions followed different paths, as they were not allowed to be direct. Its leadership wanted to adhere to the agreed contractual obligations as well as instructions regarding the export of its computers, which contained U.S. components, to third world countries.

The first act of the U.S. administration was the immediate termination of the legal outflow of technological information and knowledge from the U.S. via the company DEC to Iskra

Delta. In this context, the DEC leadership in Europe received instructions to terminate the dealership agreement with Iskra Delta in the shortest time possible and in particular to transfer the maintenance of DEC computers to a company that would not be under the influence of Iskra Delta.

The leadership of DEC managed to do this relatively quickly. They persuaded Iskra Delta's director of computer software, who then persuaded several service professionals to leave the company and, in consultation with DEC, establish their own department of representation, sales, and servicing of the imported original DEC computer equipment, which then went through the largest tourism company in Yugoslavia. Its aim was to immediately prevent the legal outflow of the DEC technology information, which the specialists of Iskra Delta received through service and other documentation.

The additional importance of this measure was that it delayed the development of Iskra Delta's computer that was compatible with the Vax processor and was based on the generic principle, which would therefore no longer be subject to the U.S. embargo. The Vax processor from DEC was also the main target of Eastern intelligence services because, at that critical time of the Cold War, the West's defensive and offensive weapons and communication systems were largely based on this computer.

In its second act, it was necessary to enlist the help of U.S. agents in Slovenia to influence the republic's leadership to replace the development oriented leadership of Iskra Delta, especially its director. The republic's leadership, on the initiative of persons who were under the influence of U.S. intelligence agencies, immediately tried to replace the director with a high party functionary, using the classic methods, but did not succeed due to the Iskra Delta workers' strong support of their director. The probable fear of a multitude of highly educated workers protesting and the fact that the company had amazing business results and a good business reputation with the public meant it was necessary to embark on another path and try to destroy the company's reputation among the public, who would then help them achieve their goals.

The third measure anticipated was the prevention of Iskra Delta's investment in the construction of a new production development centre in Ljubljana that would enable even faster development and thus even greater export opportunities abroad, particularly to the East, which was hungry at the time for Iskra Delta's products and services. New development and production capacities were based on very modern and state of the art equipment and, according to similar standards in the U.S., all of which they were able to obtain at a time when they did not represent any real danger for the West. It was also at that time one of the largest investments in Slovenia being implemented against the will of its republic's government, yet even without government support, which surprised many well-intentioned people and was unusual according to the practice at the time, Iskra Delta was able to realize its new centre.

Next, Americans intelligence agencies used the professionals working at the IBM office in Slovenia and their supporters, employed in some institutes and at the university, to begin to sow distrust within Iskra Delta and in the public about its strategy of development orientation. They essentially had to stress that it was too small to work on its own development, so they should instead rely on a large, developed American company and work for them carrying out a variety of services. As an argument, they stated that the majority of potential Yugoslav producers chose to work for one of the foreign companies in their computer business strategy, but what they did not say was precisely that such common decisions made it impossible for these companies to truly establish any development and production cooperation in the Yugoslav market.

Foreign firms were only interested in the development of such representative activities in their Yugoslav partners to generate increased sales of their products rather than those that would allow their own independent development.

For this reason, accumulations allowed by the cyclical Yugoslav computer market, unlike Iskra Delta, did not focus on strengthening their own capacity for the development of information technology, but only on consumption. This was allowed at that time through the federal laws imposed on administrative control of the importation of computers, which was not supported by a clear development strategy and therefore only led to conflict over the division of the Yugoslav market through the commission for approving the import of computers.

Upon their departure from Slovenia, the Chinese government delegation thanked the Slovenian government for the successful work of Iskra Delta in China and clearly expressed a desire for even closer cooperation with Slovenia, showing particularly great interest in development cooperation and the products and services of Iskra Delta. Soon afterward came an unexpected and sharp oral request by the president of the Slovenian political leadership to move Iskra Delta's director to a new job in the management amid the whole Iskra system. This requirement surprised the director so much that he spontaneously rejected it because he was mindful of the tasks that he still wanted to finish in the company and promises he had given to the employees, that they would complete certain projects together. This was not the first time he had been seriously threatened with consequences that would await him on account of his refusal.

One explanation for this unexpected request was probably the fact that the political leadership was frightened of the strong potential of Iskra Delta in the Chinese market, about which they spoke while the Chinese Premier was visiting, and especially of the resulting financial strength of the company because Iskra Delta's management was not politically dominated by them when it came to the company's sudden international importance.

From late 1986 until early 1987, events unfolded with lightning speed. Only a day after his rejection of departure to another job, an invitation was waiting for the director of Iskra

Delta in his office that stated that the following day he had to go to Belgrade to meet with the General Staff of the Yugoslav Army, at an address unknown to him. The General Staff of the Yugoslav Army was well known to him, since at that time the Yugoslav Army was one of their major customers, and Iskra Delta was the main sponsor of the football club Partizan. For this reason and in the belief that it was about a new job, he obligingly departed for Belgrade the next morning.

On arrival, he was in for a surprise, since those at the General Staff office did not know where the address cited in the summons was. Only when he turned to the general, who was his connection in dealings with the Army, did he learn that he was invited to see the director of the Yugoslav KOS, and the general referred him to the correct address and to the right building. The building for KOS was close to the General Staff of the Yugoslav Army's and was not known to unauthorized persons. Following procedure, he was admitted by security and taken to the premises of the director of the Yugoslav KOS, where he was welcomed by the director himself, to his great surprise, a general who was very much feared because of his power and influence over all events in former Yugoslavia.

After a short, casual talk where they got to know each other, the director of Yugoslav KOS told him that he had found out that, because of its products, Iskra Delta had caused a lot of interest abroad lately, and that there was serious danger that such interests would try to hinder its development and operations, which was, he believed, important for Yugoslavia and the Yugoslav Army.

At this meeting, the director of Iskra Delta first became aware of the activities of foreign intelligence services that had been trying to use their agents to get information on the developments and production capacities of Iskra Delta. He also learned that KOS had been closely following the developments regarding Iskra Delta ever since the acquisition of the project for the Chinese police and that, in this respect, they had already had discussions with representatives of U.S.

intelligence services in Yugoslavia regarding the achievements of Iskra Delta and the possibility that they could uncontrollably find their way out of Yugoslavia and in particular
end up in the hands of intelligence agents from the East. The
general assured him that the Americans agreed to participate,
but that they still continued to operate on their own and they
were trying, through their own people in Slovenia, to disable
the development of Iskra Delta. He also told him that even
the Eastern intelligence services were becoming more and
more aggressive in trying, together with the Chinese, different ways to get their hands on its development achievements
and to establish cooperation with Iskra Delta. The Indians,
he said, were different. They were trying to reach an agreement with Tito, Nasser, and Nehru to establish cooperation
within the Non-Aligned Movement.

Because of the sudden activities of foreign services around
Iskra Delta, the general assured him, KOS would give him
all possible support. The general also told him to expect the
highest activity of foreign intelligence services around the
construction of new production and development capacities
at Iskra Delta in Ljubljana. According to his information, the
banks in Slovenia were instructed by some of the important
politicians and party officials to impede the financing of the
construction of new facilities and to maximize the problems
of Iskra Delta's financial operations.

They arranged the way they would communicate, and the
general explained why it was important to keep the involvement of KOS and all that was said in the strictest secrecy
as long as possible. On departure, he again asserted that,
notwithstanding the pressures and intrigues certain to take
place and various attacks on him and the employees, he had
nothing to fear. However, if opponents of Iskra Delta's development launched campaigns that were too serious, he should
call him personally in the agreed manner.

The director of Iskra Delta assured him that he and his
staff would do their utmost to implement the stated objectives and that they would strongly resist any attempts to

impede development, especially now that he had the assurance that, if necessary, the relevant state bodies would help him to their full potential.

A few days after returning from Belgrade, the director of Iskra Delta received a telephone call from the Slovenian Republic Secretariat for Internal Affairs, asking him to come to the hotel at Brdo near Kranj the next day, which was the republic's protocol object under the supervision of the Secretariat for Internal Affairs. To his surprise, he found awaiting him the Republic's Secretary for Internal Affairs, who was well known to him from the time of the project for the Chinese police. The Republic's Secretary for Internal Affairs at that time was a very important and influential person in the republic. After a friendly welcome, he immediately cut to the point and explained why he had invited him in such an unusual way to the meeting at Brdo. He had heard that something strange was happening around Iskra Delta, that information came to the republic's leadership that Iskra Delta did not work well, in fact, that the results were not at all as they claimed and that they would have to take action to find a replacement if it became clear that the management did not meet Iskra Delta's planning obligations and did not listen to the instructions of the republic's leadership.

He wanted to personally find out what the truth was. The supporters of the development of Iskra Delta were reporting all this quite differently, more in line with his own positive experience gained in cooperation with Iskra Delta during the successful completion of the project in China. Because of the assurances given to the general, the director of Iskra Delta could not tell the secretary that he had been at KOS in Belgrade where he was warned that various intrigues would start occurring around Iskra Delta. He could only assure him that everything in the company was fine and that at that time the only difficulties were in acquiring the new development investment in production facilities, which some would like to prevent being built and were therefore spreading rumours about the company.

The secretary explained to him that the matter was very serious because important members of the Communist Party leadership had started to have doubts about Iskra Delta and this had caused divisions in the republic's leadership itself.

The director then had to inform the secretary of the situation at Iskra Delta and of his interview with the president of the republic's political leadership, in particular how he asked him to leave Iskra Delta and take another job in Iskra. He explained that with his determined refusal he fuelled a lot of hostility and was even threatened with consequences for not obeying the decision of the party. He told the secretary that even his explanation did not help, that given the responsibilities that he had previously assumed from the labour council of Iskra Delta, he could not leave his colleagues when they stood before brand-new challenges and unimagined opportunities for even more rapid progress both at home and abroad.

The secretary told him directly that he had not heard from the competent people about his attempted replacement, but that it certainly was not good for him and the company that he and the president of the political leadership had fallen out in such a way. He also said that these rumours about poor conditions at Iskra Delta were mainly coming from the management of Iskra, which he felt was very strange considering that they were recently praised by the republic's leadership and senior representatives of China for the company's developments and good work in China at the reception in honour of the Chinese government delegation at Brdo. At the conclusion of the meeting, they assured each other that they would do everything possible in their own areas of work to promptly determine who was really behind all this intrigue and what was really going on.

# Chapter 16

# The Attempt to Destroy Iskra Delta through the Leaders of the Iskra System

The Iskra Delta management was constantly aware, during the company's rapid growth, that without the construction of suitable and new production technology premises, they would not be able to keep up with developments in the world and compete in U.S. markets; to other companies this was a particular advantage, since they were receiving development contracts from their own governments. Iskra Delta was not able to get to the promised long-term financial assets from the very beginning, due to the influence of opponents to its development, and in particular, the agency companies that were selling foreign, mainly American, computers very profitably.

The national government promised Iskra Delta long-term loans for the resurrection of an unsuccessful attempt to manufacture computers by the then-leading companies Iskra and Gorenje, based on outdated licensing production and, therefore, not competitive on the market. The government intervened in this experiment, and by means of a special act, it instructed Iskra Delta to resurrect the previous attempts at production, but the government did not keep its promise of the long-term credit; it only interfered in the project's development on the basis of the law.

Iskra Delta was able to provide financial resources regardless of the opposition from Iskra management and certain political-economic circles in the republic, thus inducing investment in new development production capacities without a significant loss of time, an extremely important element in the rapid development of information technology. The company overcame the barriers of financing with short-term borrowing from its business partners and with advances that were paid by the contracted buyers of its computers and services to ensure priority delivery.

In return for the investment, Iskra Delta signed a turn-key contract with a company in another republic, which offered the best option for the construction of much needed development production facilities as soon as possible. This move prevented Slovenian opponents of investments in Iskra Delta from having a direct impact on the coordinated expansion of the much needed new production capacities crucial for its continued growth. When opponents of Iskra Delta's development realized they would not be able to prevent the construction of facilities that would provide even greater opportunities in the local and international markets, they started to undermine the company's public reputation through manipulation of the Iskra leadership in every possible way.

Through their connections in the republic's political leadership, the opponents organized an attack on Iskra Delta's chief financiers, who were accused by the police of working on their own account when they arranged foreign currency liquidity for Iskra Delta. This occurred during a visit of the Slovenian republic's secretary of internal affairs to the Iskra Delta Training Centre in Nova Gorica, where he himself arrived unannounced on a visit to verify the rumour that Iskra Delta was running a brothel there instead of a school. Upon completion of the visit, the secretary called the director of Iskra Delta and asked him to come to the school centre because he himself was satisfied at how happy the students were and how professional everything was, and that the rumours spread by some in Ljubljana were a complete fabrication. While the director was talking with the secretary, who also served as the head of the Slovenian police, the police force, without his knowledge, as he said in his later statement, seized two of the Iskra Delta financiers and members of the commission for the import of computers from Belgrade under the accusation that they stole money from the company. All three were detained in prison in Koper.

The director of Iskra Delta learned only the next morning that these employees were not at work because they were imprisoned under the accusation of theft. Immediately, he called the secretary for republic internal affairs, who explained to him that these people had been stealing money for quite a long time during foreign exchange transactions. It was clear to him at once why the arrest of the financiers had happened, as Iskra Delta was at that time at its most vulnerable because of large investments. Precisely because of this, the director was not hesitant, and he headed to the prison in Koper at once, with the head of legal services. The governor did not allow anyone to talk to the imprisoned colleagues at first, saying that such were his instructions from Ljubljana. He only relented when the director threatened to inform all journalists accredited in Ljubljana that the police were not fulfilling their duty of providing legal protection to his colleagues who were jailed without a formal charge. The three were visibly affected, and in very poor condition, but were firmly convinced that it had all been a mistake. The director, after his return to Ljubljana, immediately began a campaign to get them released from prison as soon as possible.

After a brief discussion of the situation with the KOS director, it was clear to the director of Iskra Delta that this was only the beginning of a more extensive campaign, directed primarily against the leadership of Iskra Delta. The first continuation followed in the form of an ordered article in the republic's main newspaper on how Iskra Delta stole social resources and how its management was doing nothing to control the situation (because Iskra Delta was developing and expanding too fast without the consent of the Iskra management). Shortly after the publication of other articles about developments related to Iskra Delta, the president of the Iskra Board convened a meeting in Cankarjev dom of all leading people in the Iskra company, headed by party secretaries, chairmen of trade unions for companies, and presidents of the workers' councils. This meeting, attended by hundreds of leading individuals of Iskra, was also attended by some leading members of the republic's government and some of the republic's party leaders. Because of its announced importance, the national television and some selected journalists from all of the republic's major media were preparing to report on it.

Already, during the opening speech of the president of the Iskra Board, it was clear that he would not be talking about the development of Iskra as a whole, but only about the fact that they had within the system a company whose activities were destroying the reputation and development of Iskra as a whole. After this attack by the president of Iskra on Iskra Delta, some began to look maliciously at Iskra Delta delegates. They expected an even worse attack to follow as the head of the republic's party stepped up to the platform to talk.

The director of Iskra Delta was ready to speak and, if necessary, to reject all the allegations uttered by the president of the party. But the expected attack did not happen. The president of the party spoke only in general and made no accusations against Iskra Delta, as had been expected by the Iskra leadership, especially its president. After the speech by the president of the party, an awkwardness filled the hall because those present no longer knew why they had been gathered, and the president of Iskra was so surprised that he could find nothing more to say. Most likely, he realized that while he was speaking, something had happened which prevented the intended plan from being carried out.

This situation was resolved when the composed president of Iskra trade unions thanked everyone in a short speech for the business results achieved during the previous year and closed the meeting. People were leaving Cankarjev dom visibly angry because they found it inconceivable that they had had to leave their work for something as inane as what they had just heard.

The director of Iskra Delta was outraged and went to the Iskra head office, where he found the Iskra president and several of the republic's leadership drinking whiskey and looking stunned that he had turned up there. Upon seeing him, some of them almost dropped their glasses. Without waiting for an invitation to join them, he first scolded the president of Iskra, asking how he dared to attack Iskra Delta and its leadership without having any proof. As the president of Iskra could never expect that someone would accuse him so directly, and in front of the republic's party leadership, he just mumbled an answer and left the president of the party to resolve the matter, who offered a glass of whiskey to the director of Iskra Delta and turned the situation into a joke.

After that conflict with the leadership of Iskra, who were working in collusion with some of the republic's officials, an organized underground operation by the Iskra leadership against the leadership of Iskra Delta began in order to prevent the timely completion of their new facilities. They did not have to choose the means of achieving this; it was done for them. Good interpersonal relations within the team, successful and rapid development, and good personal income at the time meant that Iskra Delta executives had great support from employees. So Iskra Delta's opponents decided to engage them at the one point where they expected the employees to stop supporting the leadership. They did everything possible to prevent the timely payment of personal income and salaries in Iskra Delta, believing that when the employees did not get their salaries on time, they would change the director and his closest associates themselves. To this end, the directors of the banks in Slovenia with whom Iskra Delta worked received secret instructions to disrupt the financial operations of Iskra Delta.

Because the director of Iskra Delta was informed about this in due time, he called the KOS director, who assured him that the money for personal salaries would be paid to Iskra Delta's account in time and that he should be more concerned that the work continue smoothly in the company.

The director of Iskra Delta was aware that without accurately informing as many employees as possible in time regarding what was happening around Iskra Delta, it would not be possible to prevent the long-term plots by its opponents; therefore, before the employees were to be paid, he convened an assembly of all employees in the largest cinema in Ljubljana, bringing together employees from all work processes of Iskra Delta in Slovenia as well as representatives of Delta offices all over Yugoslavia. During the assembly, before the director's speech, the atmosphere was very strained, as the Iskra management had planted some people there who managed to disseminate misinformation and stir unrest among the workers, saying that without replacing the director, their salaries would not be paid, according to what they were told at the headquarters of Iskra.

The director was aware of his responsibilities in giving such a performance; in more than an hour-long speech, he told the employees what was happening. He clearly informed them that some people in the republic wanted to prevent the development of computer science based on self-developed solutions and that they were demanding Iskra Delta rely on one of the foreign companies as its subcontractor in its development. He also said that the leadership of Iskra Delta did not intend to bow to this pressure, that they were not alone on this journey, and that due to the company's good business results in line with inflation, personal income would be increased by 15 percent and paid on time. When referring to the increase in personal income during that time of frozen salaries, he further mobilized the employees to resist attempts to impede development.

Provocateurs hired by the Iskra executives were surprised by the strong onset of the director's vision and strategic development, so that after his speech they lay low. They were greatly shocked when he received a tremendous amount of applause, and assurances by some employees that they would, if necessary, even work free of charge. But victory over their opponents was not yet certain, especially with this kind of ending to the meeting. The director still had to persuade his colleagues in the financial sector that, regardless of the fact that they did not have enough money in their account, they execute the calculation of salaries on computer magnetic tape and deliver it to the agreed place at the republic SDK, which was then responsible for checking and payment of personal income. From there, everything depended on whether the promised money would arrive on the account of Iskra Delta in time to pay personal salaries, as was promised at the workers assembly. The hours prior to payment passed with everybody in the company feeling very anxious, particularly the director, who was the only one who knew what was going on in the background.

Everything took place as agreed, and information on the payment of salaries began to arrive at the Iskra Delta plants before the end of the working day. Once received by the employees, an indescribable enthusiasm overcame everybody, especially when they saw that they really had received the 15 percent raise they were promised by the director and because they knew that salaries were frozen in other parts of Iskra. Following this payment, working zeal increased dramatically, and those few workers the Iskra management was using to cause unrest and spread misinformation temporarily kept their heads down.

The payment of salaries, and especially the raise, resulted in a storm within the leadership of Iskra and among politicians because they did not know who had made it possible for Iskra Delta to receive the money in time. Even more, they became suspicious because they did not know who in their scheme was not sticking to the given instructions. They could not conceive of such a scenario, because at that time, no director had ever blatantly resisted politics in such a way without being punished at least by losing his job.

Since Iskra Delta had the majority of the market and customers in the other republics of former Yugoslavia, the opponents convinced themselves that one of its major customers must have given the money, but they were not able to determine who because even then the relations between the republics, especially with the federal government, were not very friendly, even to the point of trying to do harm to one another. The opponents orchestrated a similar scenario to prevent the payroll being paid the next month, and they further influenced Iskra Delta's customers in Slovenia not to make any payments before the delivery of equipment and services, saying that Iskra Delta, due to liquidity problems, would not be able to meet its obligations to them. The most important customers were informed that this complication was due to Iskra Delta's heavy investment in borrowed money on the grey market, so buyers in Slovenia largely accepted and took these warnings into account.

The money for personal income came from an unknown source the second time, so that Iskra Delta again paid its workers' salaries on time and satisfied its obligations to its customers with minimum delay. Opponents started to panic, especially those in the leadership of Iskra, because of Iskra Delta's continued smooth operation and because they had no idea who it was in Slovenia and Yugoslavia that was backing them. Even the directors of other Iskra companies began to visit directors' meetings and request clarification from the Iskra leadership about the rumours of what was happening at Iskra Delta.

At one such directors' meeting, the director of Iskra Delta succeeded, notwithstanding the opposition of the leadership, in explaining what was happening in Iskra Delta and, without beating around the bush, said who it was behind the whole conspiracy against them and their investment in the new plant. The president of Iskra said that the accusations by the Iskra Delta director were untrue, but most directors of the other Iskra companies believed the Iskra Delta director, as they themselves saw that no matter what happened around Iskra Delta, the new plant construction was progressing rapidly.

Gradually, the intrigue surrounding Iskra Delta took effect, stealing time and much needed energy, and becoming increasingly more difficult to resist. It caused real financial problems, so much so that in May 1987, the management decided to prepare an extensive report for the working council of Iskra Delta (the highest managing authority) titled "The Development of the Domestic Industry of Computer Science so Far and Proposals for Measures to Achieve the Strategic Objectives in the Field of Information Technology." The council adopted the report as its own and sent it to the most influential authorities in the republic with a request to support the efforts of Iskra Delta in overcoming problems and to put an end to the external pressures then being implemented with the tacit consent of some members of the current political leadership in Slovenia.

This came through only after the informal and unplanned visit by the most influential politician in Slovenia to Iskra Delta's school centre and the informal talk between the president of the republic's government in Nova Gorica and an important general of the Yugoslav Army. This general, who was invited by the president, came to the school centre in the middle of 1987 and managed to persuade the president of the republic's government, in front of the attending representatives from Iskra Delta, of the importance of Iskra Delta for Yugoslavia's international reputation and the modernization of the Yugoslav Army, and made a point of requesting the immediate end to the pressures on Iskra Delta and its development. At the meeting, he clearly expressed the position of the Army, and that the development of Iskra Delta was in the strategic interests of national defence.

The president of the republic's government said at the meeting that he would personally support the development of Iskra Delta. The first result of this was that the falsely imprisoned financiers were gradually released, naturally without an apology for the time they were wrongly detained. Soon the pressures on Iskra Delta stopped, so that they could, without major complications, complete the construction of the new development production facilities by the end of that year.

The opening and acquisition of this modern technology facility in early December 1987 was very modest, yet festive.

This development manufacturing centre was built entrepreneurially, without the usual state support, which was difficult for many to believe. On seeing the factory, the attending experts were unanimous that it would represent a quality milestone in the development of Iskra Delta and computer science in Slovenia and the region.

The republic's highest officials did not attend the opening ceremony, only the president of the Republic Committee for Science and Technology, who was one of the few people in the republic's government to openly support Iskra Delta in its development efforts on every occasion. The attending journalists wrote about this absence with amazement because, in those days, important politicians usually gathered in full numbers at the openings of even small manufacturing plants. The leadership of the university, the president of the Academy of Arts and Sciences, and senior military representatives were also present. The biggest shock of all was the attendance and speech by the president of the business committee for Iskra; because of the praise by the professional public and those present at the opening, he tried to alleviate the problems that he had directly caused for Iskra Delta in the completion of the construction of the factory.

The opening was welcomed by the employees, since this acquisition gave them the real possibility of even faster, high-quality development. With the new facilities, they were given the opportunity to raise the quality of products in all processes, from development through production to sales and installation for users worldwide, none of which they could achieve before due to inadequate and fragmented production capacity. Up to then, with artificial and aging computers, they could not introduce a new technological production process that would allow the control of the input of reproductive materials in the production sub-phases, and at the end test the produced systems in special chambers under different climatic conditions to identify any weak points of the new product before delivery. Now they could supply users with more reliable machines while incurring lower costs themselves because they were able to reduce the service interventions.

The results of working in the new premises were already evident the following year, as they received many awards for quality from users, the most important one being at the fair in Leipzig, where Iskra Delta was the only company among the exhibitors to receive the gold award for technological achievement, quality, and design for its PC Trident (Triglav); it was also voted best product at the fair.

Having failed to prevent the construction of the factory, some of the opponents, obviously, found themselves on the wrong side as a result of influence from abroad, so they again kept a low profile. Even the republic leadership sought to salvage its reputation after choosing to be absent at the opening of the factory; this is why they gathered in such large numbers to celebrate the tenth anniversary of Iskra Delta in Cankarjev dom, where the president of the republic greeted the attending Delta employees and all the other invited guests.

In his speech, he praised the achievements of Iskra Delta in development but noted that tough times awaited the company before being ejected from the secret ring, which certain foreign powers had made to stop its further development. He also emphasized how important the field of information technologies was for Slovenia and Yugoslavia, and that it was this new knowledge industry in which Iskra Delta was progressing, despite all obstacles.

Iskra Delta took advantage of this celebration in particular to motivate its employees even more by awarding the most deserving Delta employees and the major users of its systems and solutions, and to improve its reputation with the public, which was rather shaken by the backdoor tricks during the building of the factory. Indeed, the reputation of Iskra Delta greatly improved among the public after the opening of the Delta factory and especially after the high-profile celebration of its tenth anniversary.

The battle for a superior position and market conquest resumed. Through one of the Iskra companies in Slovenia,

IBM's local representation made an offer to the Iskra management for Yugoslavia to assemble an IBM personal computer
in direct competition with the well-selling Delta computer
Partner. The offer was published in the media, but IBM did
not take it seriously, as it soon turned out; consequently the
assembly did not occur in the Iskra company. This episode
only caused confusion in the market, as IBM representatives
claimed to their customers that Iskra Delta would support the
production of their PC, because it would stop the production
of its Partner personal computer, which was not based on the
MS-DOS operating system. Iskra Delta responded quickly to
this and published a MS-DOS operating system on its Triglav computer, averting any significant damage to the Yugoslav PC market, and users then had both operating systems,
CP/M and MS-DOS, at their disposal.

Soon after the failed announcement campaign for IBM
PC production with Iskra, Iskra Delta management received
an offer from the IBM representatives in Europe stating that
IBM would like to begin production of their minicomputer
System 400 using their premises, noting that it was not in
direct competition with the Iskra Delta's product range and
would only be an addition to the market according to customer requirements. It was immediately clear to the Iskra
Delta leadership that behind this desire was a wish to get a
better view of what was happening behind the walls of the
new plant, but Iskra Delta accepted the offer and sent two of
its experts to the technological development and production
seminar at a similar IBM factory in Italy. Upon their return,
they reported that the cooperation with IBM might result
in the full capacity of the new factory with the project's additional programs, but they saw that IBM, under the guise
of production, only carried out final configuration testing of
computer systems in Italy before delivery to customers in Europe. The Iskra Delta management realized that IBM wanted
to import the whole computer under the guise of assembly,
thus avoiding Yugoslavian restrictions on equipment import,

and that this was not tied to a commitment to increase exports by the buyer.

Soon it became clear that the IBM representative agency in Yugoslavia had tried through this offer to Iskra Delta to kill two birds with one stone, as they would on the one hand satisfy the requirement of U.S. intelligence services to hinder the development of Iskra Delta, and at the same time increase the sales of their machines in the market through supposed production in Yugoslavia. With this realization, Iskra Delta management accepted the game and agreed to sign a contract with IBM on the production of the IBM System 400 series of computers, as it was aware that it was better to cooperate with IBM in the market than to oppose it head-on. In this way, Iskra Delta was able to offer computers from the two largest U.S. computer companies, IBM and DEC, making it unique in the world at that time.

At that moment, the interest of KGB agents in the happenings in and around Iskra Delta suddenly escalated.

During these market games, the Iskra Delta leadership was unaware of the real intentions behind the two American companies, of course, which were likely coordinated to work as instructed by the U.S. administration: to have Iskra Delta as much as possible under their supervision, and in particular, to observe what was going on in their development departments so that the technology, which was then mastered, would not come into the hands of the Eastern agents who were quite willing to use any means necessary to obtain it. At that time, the two U.S. firms also took turns attempting to influence Iskra Delta's key experts to be recruited by IBM or DEC. This was reflected in the work atmosphere, as they were promised increased salaries and education in the U.S., not only in one but in the other company, as well. In addition to spreading misinformation within the company itself, this was the most effective attack on the development of Iskra Delta, and due to events in Yugoslavia at the time, the Iskra Delta leadership was unable to successfully deal with it.

# Chapter 17

# The Interview of the Iskra Delta Director with the President of the Indian Government, Rajiv Gandhi

Iskra Delta's success in China, based on creating the computer network for the Chinese police in very short time and linking eight major Chinese cities with each other in an integrated system, had become common knowledge and something of great interest in neighbouring India. Shortly after completion of the installation in China, the Indian Embassy, through a daughter of a high diplomat in Belgrade, established contacts with experts at Iskra Delta to see for themselves, informally, what they were doing and what their abilities were in the field of information technology. Not long after, they announced their desire to work with Iskra Delta on projects as specialists in software. Once the Iskra Delta executives had assessed the experience the Indians had, they agreed to cooperate, which quickly resulted in the Indian Ambassador to Yugoslavia himself announcing an informal visit to Iskra Delta in Ljubljana.

They were well prepared for this visit, and the ambassador and his colleagues, after the introductory presentation of the organization and strategy of the company, expressed the desire for an immediate visit to the school centre in Nova Gorica, having heard of the modern methods Iskra Delta was using to transfer knowledge in the information technology field to its users. At the time, this school was the centre of a very modern demonstration complex where Iskra Delta could show and demonstrate its products and software solutions to prospective buyers in one place, which was crucial for the acquisition of major projects and transactions.

An excellent demonstration of products and solutions was prepared and presented to the ambassador and his staff, making a great impression on all the Indians They did not conceal their surprise at the fact that, in a small country such as Yugoslavia, a developed modern company could exist that managed technology in time periods so short as one could only get in the U.S. at the time. The Americans did not permit access of the latest technology in computer science to India at the time of the Cold War, so it was all the more important for the ambassador that he found a company in politically friendly Yugoslavia that had the knowledge and had mastered these technologies that his country was so interested in. The ambassador promised the Iskra Delta director before leaving that he would immediately inform Prime Minister Rajiv Gandhi what he had seen, because he knew that, as an engineer himself, he was very interested in the development of computer technology and its introduction in the Indian economy.

Shortly after the visit of the Indian Ambassador to Nova Gorica, Iskra Delta was invited to exhibit its products at the International Fair in New Delhi and to present its achievements to the widest possible circle of Indian professionals. At this fair at the beginning of 1988, Iskra Delta presented its computers Partner and Trident. In particular, the Trident, with its configuration of the Motorola 68000 processor and the Unix operating system, impressed the Indian experts the most, as they had no opportunity to see a similar computer with such capabilities due to the U.S. embargo on India. Early on at the fair, various Indian companies and individual experts in business began to suggest doing business with Iskra Delta. Everybody was most interested in writing applications based on the Unix operating system for potential users in India and in countries where Iskra Delta planned to sell its Trident. During his visit to the fair, Congressional President

Author talks with India's President Radjiv Gandhi

Gandhi of India lingered at the Iskra Delta exhibition for a long time, where an expert presented and demonstrated the capabilities of the Trident computer in detail at his request, followed by public praise and thanks by the president to the specialist who conducted this successful presentation so professionally.

The Indian state delegation headed by Prime Minister Rajiv Gandhi arrived in Yugoslavia that same year to a warm and friendly reception. Both countries were leaders in the Non-Aligned Movement, and the Indian president gave, shortly after arrival, a resounding speech in the Yugoslav Federal Assembly, in which he primarily advocated technology cooperation among the Non-Aligned countries. He stressed the need for India, Egypt, and Yugoslavia to be the driving forces in this strategically important area and to fulfil the agreement reached between the presidents Nehru, Nasser, and Tito. This agreement stressed not only political cooperation of the Non-Aligned countries but also cooperation in the technological, economic, and military fields.

The Yugoslav government at the time was very favourably inclined toward this initiative, but did not include Iskra Delta among the builders of this cooperation on the Yugoslav side because, at that time, it was not aware of Iskra Delta's potential and because it generally favoured traditional industries. Before leaving Yugoslavia, the Indian Prime Minister prepared a reception in his residence for members of the Yugoslav government, the diplomatic corps, and important businessmen. An invitation to this reception was also given to the director of Iskra Delta, to his great surprise, and it was indicated from the Indian side that President Gandhi would want to talk to him personally about the achievements of Iskra Delta and to hear from him about his vision for further development of information technology at Iskra Delta.

What happened next at the reception is a true account. The president, after the official part of the reception was over, met with the director of Iskra Delta alone, which caused confusion among some members of the Yugoslav delegation, since they did not know the Indian intelligence service in Yugoslavia had accurately informed him about the technological capabilities of Iskra Delta. For Iskra Delta, this represented great recognition from India for its developments in information technology. In a short, relaxed interview, the two discussed the president's request as engineers; the director presented the strategic development in the direction of parallel computer processing and, among other things, the PARSYS project. For this project, the president showed particularly strong interest and immediately suggested that its development include relevant Indian institutes and universities. He saw immediate possibility for successful cooperation in the fact that Indian experts could be involved at once in the Iskra Delta projects, mainly in the field of software, since both India and Yugoslavia together could offer technological solutions to other, mainly Non-Aligned countries. They agreed that for immediate cooperation, the best basis was Iskra Delta's latest computer system, the Trident, for which the software for different applications would be produced by the Indians, but the system itself would be produced and developed by Iskra Delta, and later, its production could be held as a joint venture in India.

The director of Iskra Delta was surprised that President Gandhi knew all the Trident's capacities in detail, and was therefore all the more appreciative of his praise for this technological achievement. He was even happier about his statement that this system would have many users in India in various fields. In the interview, they especially emphasized the importance of educating the professionals for the use and development of computer technology in the various fields of the economy.

They agreed to an immediate visit by Iskra Delta professionals to India to establish direct contacts with the relevant Indian institutes and companies so that the cooperation could begin as soon as possible. The president also proposed that Iskra Delta establish a joint venture company in India as soon as possible, which would serve as the foundation for the fulfilment of the agreements reached in Belgrade. The president of India was visibly pleased after the meeting and invited the director of Iskra Delta to visit India himself as soon as possible to see for himself the achievements and abilities of his great country and its people.

When leaving the interview, the director of Iskra Delta was escorted by the president's adjutant, who had been constantly in the background writing down everything that was said at the meeting. The members of the Yugoslav government at the reception were very interested in the conversation because they could not understand why the president of such an important country devoted so much time to a director of a relatively small company. The director of Iskra Delta thus briefly reported on the content of the interview and expressed hope that the Yugoslav government would be far more supportive in further development. Some present gave him frank recognition of the success; others said that he was not authorized to hold discussion at such a high level, mostly because they were envious that Iskra Delta held such a strong perception in India.

Fortunately for Iskra Delta, the initiative for cooperation was given by the Indians, which was also evident at the meeting of the Yugoslav-Indian joint committee for economic cooperation, where Iskra Delta officially presented its capacities to the Indian government delegation, led by their Minister of Commerce on a visit to Yugoslavia. The result of this presentation was a committee decision that Iskra Delta's technology should become the basis of cooperation between Yugoslavia and India in the field of computer science.

Iskra Delta, according to this decision, undertook immediate action to implement these important and complex tasks without delay toward the fulfilment of the promised huge potentials in India and in the Non-Aligned countries. Visits of its experts to India were successful, since the Indians welcomed them openly, and the agreements were quickly completed. Committed and without bureaucratic complications, they immediately prepared everything for the registration of a joint venture company of Iskra Delta in India. Enthusiasm of the experts on both sides instilled great optimism during the initial stages of work and deepened mutual cooperation, as the Indians were hungry to work with computers, which for the most part they lacked. The ones they did have were in rare, specialized universities and institutes.

Indian recognition that Trident was ideally suited for extensive use in India gave the leadership of Iskra Delta additional arguments that, by relying on long-term and strategic cooperation with this great country, they were on the right track. They were supported by the leaders of India, who represented tremendous opportunities for more than one hundred million educated people in successful mutual development. Iskra Delta did not have such support in Yugoslavia, as the joint country had already started to disintegrate, and the Yugoslav government looked on the agreements reached with India with its fingers crossed behind its back, knowing that success would allow Iskra Delta and its partners tremendous development.

Instead of immediate support as promised in the agreements with India, the government, due to inter-republic conflict, demanded unification of computer development on the national level in Yugoslavia first, and in such a way that all the republics would be satisfied. This, of course, was impossible to achieve and was something all the players were well aware of. Nevertheless, they insisted on these unrealistic demands, which inhibited development of Iskra Delta and harmed the good relations with India.

# Chapter 18

# Star Wars—a Threat by the U.S. President to the Soviet Union Regarding Intelligent Missiles

President Reagan of the U.S. and Soviet Union President Gorbachev were the main players in the Cold War in the eighties. They met five times between 1985 and 1988. The initiative for these meetings was given by U.S. President Reagan because the CIA had better managed the situation in the Soviet Union than the KGB had in the U.S. The nature of this war was exhausting for both of them in their race for nuclear weapons advantages and, in this respect, also their competition in the development of rocket technology and in space. This silent war was led by their operational espionage agents, who often became the real and direct victims of this war. The effects of this war primarily meant economic depletion on both sides, but because of their economic superiority, the Americans found it easier to tolerate than the Soviets. New technologies in all areas were rapidly developing in this war as by-products, but the information technologies were the most significant in the U.S.

The Americans gambled all their resources from the outset on the development of information technologies, since they knew this would be the key to progress in all other fields. As it turned out, they were correct. In contrast, the Soviet Union neglected this field from the outset and later realized it was already too late. Its next big mistake was in trying to make up for the lag with the Americans through its agents in the West by theft of information on technology achievements. These

169

fatal errors were largely responsible for the Soviet Union losing the Cold War.

When the Americans saw the efforts in the East to catch up with them, they opted for a strict embargo on the export of products in the field of information technology from Western countries. The Soviets tried to make up for their lag in process automation and accuracy with the strategy of hitting targets with larger quantities of atomic weapons and better missiles, but this was neither sufficient nor effective in the competition over armaments with the Americans. On the contrary, this trend in increasing the number of weapons but not their accuracy and quality only further exhausted them economically and led to the realization that they needed major reforms to their system and outlook.

With the election of Reagan as the president of the U.S., the Cold War was exacerbated because he chose a strategy of even greater economic depletion to the Soviet Union with the announcement of a technologically and economically challenging project: Star Wars. A major role in this project was played by the significant advantage the U.S. had in the development and production of information technologies and standards, which were, of course, determined by the leading U.S. companies in the development of this field in the world. The Americans were well aware that this had to be timely and effectively used.

The Soviet Union, because of its desire to catch up with the U.S. as quickly as possible, decided on yet another wrong move: copying the IBM System 360 and the DEC PDP 11 computers. When the Americans found out what the Soviets were doing, they wisely took advantage of the situation and planted them with viruses and modified parts, further crippling the development of information technology in the Soviet Union and thus the possibility of using computers in their weapons and industrial systems. The strategy of maximizing the economic depletion of the Soviet Union was probably the reason Americans set the prices of their computer equipment so high during the Cold War; this ranged from a few hundred thousand to several million U.S. dollars, depending on the speed and configuration.

Even U.S.-allied countries, where U.S. computer companies were allowed to export, had to pay up to 50 percent more than in the U.S. Soviet agents were forced to pay still larger amounts if they wanted to buy a computer or its components on the black market. The day had come when the opposing leaders of the Cold War had to meet as a result of the effectiveness of the U.S. strategy to deplete the economies of its opponents.

They first met in November 1985 in Geneva and then again in Reykjavik in 1986, to agree on the withdrawal of missiles from Europe. These talks were not successful, so the Americans threatened the Soviets with accelerated armaments and with their new Star Wars project while emphasizing that their weak and underdeveloped economy would not last if they wanted to follow them in armaments. Soviet President Gorbachev soon found out that it would not be possible with increased spending on armaments to carry out the planned economic reforms called Perestroika and the social reforms called Glasnost, with which he tried to introduce more democracy in the country. He was concerned with how to keep the members of the Warsaw Pact under control if economic conditions worsened due to increased investments in armaments, so in further talks, the Soviets indicated their willingness to relax their nuclear arms program, which quickly led to the first signing of a relevant agreement.

Furthermore, the Soviets still tried very hard to respond to the U.S. Star Wars project, which meant even greater economic depletion of the Soviet Union because they did not have a developed and appropriate industrial technology base to respond effectively to this challenge. The Americans, on the contrary, advanced such technology even more in this period, as they produced their own computers for the whole world, which increasingly established the standards and formed the basis for the automation industry and defence systems.

The role of computers was most important in the defensive and offensive military systems developed by the Americans and on which Reagan's threat with intelligent missiles was based when he visited Moscow. They knew all too well that the Soviets could not effectively respond to this challenge because of their problems in the field of information technology. Successfully planted, corrupt Western computer components did their part, and all copies of Western computers in different countries of the Eastern Bloc were controlled by U.S. agents. The Soviets were horrified to realize that the computers they produced were completely unreliable and that their use in their latest weapons and production systems resulted in even greater casualties and damage to themselves.

The realization that they had misread the developments in information technology, that such technology, because of the rapid development in the U.S., was becoming increasingly important in all fields of labour and management, that the Americans were indirectly controlling their computer production in the East and that U.S. intelligence agencies managed to plant computer assemblies and sub-assemblies intended for sale in the East with viruses caused considerable panic and despondency in the leadership of the Soviet Union.

Probably for this reason, U.S. President Reagan and his colleagues were able to convince President Gorbachev and his colleagues during their visit to Moscow in May 1988 that the Soviet Union would not be able to withstand a precise computer and satellite-guided U.S. missile attack in the case of a mutual conflict. In contrast, the Americans showed that when the Star Wars project was complete, they would be able to shoot down Soviet missiles with nuclear warheads before they even left Soviet territory.

During the talks between the two presidents, Gorbachev was undoubtedly in an inferior position as he realized that the East did not have computers and related systems with which they could adequately respond to the Americans. This is why the Soviet President started to give in to the

Americans' requirements more and more. The biggest irony in all this was that Yugoslavia had a small company that was running a promotion for their own computers in the immediate vicinity of the Kremlin, where talks were held between the Soviets and Americans, claiming that their computers could perfectly replace the U.S. computers.

# Chapter 19

## The Visit by the President of the Soviet Union Mikhail Gorbachev to Slovenia— Presentation of the Achievements of Iskra Delta

The Soviet leadership's opponents of appeasement in relations with the U.S. convinced President Gorbachev to visit Yugoslavia in March of 1988 with the primary purpose of visiting a few leading Slovenian companies in the field of information technology in Europe, then seeing the Iskra setup in Ljubljana, of which a major part was the associated Iskra Delta company. Under the guise of an exchange of views with the Slovenian party leadership about socialist development paths, the main purpose of the visit by the Soviet delegation was hidden: for them to see for themselves what the Yugoslav Republic could offer the Soviet Union in the field of strategic technologies, where they fatally lagged behind in development with their allies compared to the U.S. and its allies.

The Soviet KGB was present with its agents in Slovenia and knew very well that the most technologically advanced and therefore most important interests for the Soviet Union were the following Iskra companies: Mikroelektronika, Elektro Optika, Telematika, and especially Iskra Delta. Therefore, the leadership of the republic's party in Slovenia was informed that the Soviet side wished for President Gorbachev and his colleagues to see not only how far Slovenia had advanced in the socialist form of social development, but how far along

President of Soviet Union Mr. Mihail Gorbachov
greating for demonstration of Trident

the Slovenian companies were in the development of the latest information technologies. This meant it was essential to
visit the largest Slovenian company at the time, Iskra. The
Slovenian party leadership gladly allowed everything, so the
mentioned Iskra companies at the request of the republic
communist party leadership had to prepare presentations of
their newest products for the Soviet delegation.

The Slovenian leadership probably did not know then the
real purpose of the visit of the Soviet delegation, and they
thought the Soviets were primarily interested in the development of socialist self-management in Yugoslavia, especially in
Slovenia, and that the requirement to visit Iskra was only a
courtesy. The Soviet Union was at that time in a very difficult economic situation and in an increasingly weak and also
largely lost position in its relations with the U.S. This was further impeded because they realized the Americans had planted

corrupt components in the production of their own computers –something that even the KGB knew nothing about at the
beginning. In preparing the visit of the Soviet delegation to
Yugoslavia, KGB agents had the last word, and this is why the
Yugoslav KOS played an active part in all events.

The relations between the republics in the former Yugoslavia and the Federation were strained at that time, and the
KOS director did not trust most of the republics' leaderships.
This was why hardly anyone in Slovenia was informed about
the true purpose of the visit by the Soviet delegation. The
KOS director told the director of Iskra Delta that the American intelligence service, the CIA, was certainly more familiar
with the real purpose of the visit and that was why they expressed to KOS the desire for the director of Iskra Delta to
remain passive during the visit and to not attend the presentation of the developments and abilities of Iskra Delta to the
Soviet delegation.

The Americans expressed this wish because, probably,
based on the experience with the presentation in Washington,
they feared that the director of Iskra Delta would address the
Soviet delegation overly optimistically and, if possible, ensure that the Soviets could catch up to the Americans in the
field of information technologies with the help of Yugoslavia,
which could lead to strengthened and further resistance and
insistence of the Soviet Union in the economically debilitat-
ing race in the Cold War with the Americans and their allies.

The KOS general, also probably for his own reasons,
wanted to help the Americans with their wish and, accordingly, gave appropriate instructions to the director of Iskra
Delta. He advised against participation in the presentation
of the Iskra Delta's accomplishments to the Soviet president
and informed him of the scheduled plan. He said that the
director would be visited by his secret confidant, who would
give him a special injection in his office, after which he would
get a high fever, so that the KGB agents would not be suspicious as to why he did not attend the presentation to the Soviet delegation as was expected.

In this sensitive period of the Cold War, when the main role was played by the intelligence services, the KGB agents certainly learned about the arrangements between the CIA and KOS. For this reason, they wanted to have the director of Iskra Delta under their supervision to ensure that he would take part in the presentation and present the developments and strategy for the further development of Iskra Delta to the president and members of the delegation. Above all, they wanted to be certain that he would be ready to talk about development cooperation with the relevant Soviet companies that would be proposed by the Soviet delegation and the possibility of immediate transfer of the technological achievements of Iskra Delta to the Soviet Union.

Chances are this was why the Soviets sent two KGB agents to Iskra Delta, announced as special envoys of President Gorbachev, to tell him in private what the president expected of the talk with him at the scheduled presentation of the achievements of Iskra Delta regarding joint development opportunities with Eastern institutes and companies. They especially emphasized that the collaboration of Iskra Delta in joint development of information technologies with Soviet institutes and companies had additional importance if they wanted to get free passage and special benefits for the further penetration of their products and services on their huge market. This cooperation would also be extraordinarily important for further economic development and friendly relations with Yugoslavia, and especially with Slovenia.

The Iskra Delta director told the agents immediately and clearly that they would cooperate with them only in such a manner as not to violate agreements with the Americans, because in their products they used American technology and components of American companies that were subject to embargo. The agents were visibly disappointed and said that Iskra Delta was a Yugoslav company, and should act independently and decide with whom and how they would cooperate, and the Soviets would agree on all the rest themselves with the Yugoslav government. After this brief but intense talk, they said that they would wait for him in the secretary's office, stating that they were charged with the task of accompanying him to the scheduled presentation and interview with President Gorbachev.

KOS was informed in time about the presence of KGB agents at Iskra Delta, which is why the special agent in charge of "disabling" the director of Iskra Delta temporarily came to his office through the side doors not associated with the secretary's office and quickly gave him the injection.

It had an immediate effect, so the director called a driver immediately after the departure of the KOS agent to take him to a doctor. The KGB agents immediately assumed there was something wrong, and wanted to prevent his departure from the office, but when they saw that he was practically burning with fever, they gave in and the director was taken to the agreed location.

The presentation of Iskra's achievements to the Soviet delegation, which consisted of experts in the field of information technology, was held without the director of Iskra Delta; consequently, the level of information did not meet the expectations of the colleagues of the Soviet president. The content of the presentation itself, though, by the Iskra Delta experts, especially the display of the capabilities of the Triglav computer and its design, did make a big impression on the members of the delegation. The enthusiasm of many members of the delegation increased due to the knowledge that a small country like Yugoslavia had made such technological advancements in such a short period of time.

Some prominent members of the Soviet delegation posed such technical questions to the Iskra specialists that it soon turned out that most members of the delegation had a better understanding of information technology than their understanding of the problems of socialist development, which was supposedly the reason why they visited Slovenia in the first place. The surprise was even greater for the Soviets when they found out that everything showed by Iskra Delta was achieved on the company's own self initiative, without a national plan or the related support, and that Iskra Delta did not receive money for the development of products from the state, but had to earn it on the market. It was unthinkable for the members of the delegation because they knew something like that simply could not happen in the Soviet system.

During the talks with representatives of Iskra after the presentation, the members of the Soviet delegation, with the consent of the president, expressed the belief that after their return to Moscow they would do everything in their power to make sure that the Iskra technology would start to be used as quickly and widely as possible for the development of the Soviet Union. At the same time, they stressed that they were interested in further joint development of information technologies with the relevant companies in the Soviet Union on the basis of long-term cooperation, for which they were ready to sign corresponding agreements with the Yugoslav government.

But probably none of the members on the Yugoslav side highlighted to the Soviet delegation during the talks that many of the Iskra products, especially those of Iskra Delta, were subject to the U.S. government export licenses in order to export to the Eastern Bloc countries. It is likely that the KGB agents came to the conclusion that only the leadership of Iskra Delta, headed by its director, adhered to the agreements with the Americans and that this was not the policy of the Yugoslav government.

But precisely because the leadership of Iskra Delta consistently adhered to the agreements with the U.S. administration, the acquisition of licenses for exports to the East based on the End Use Certificates could run relatively smoothly and quickly, which was already confirmed in practice by the Delta computers exported to the Soviet Union, Poland, and Czechoslovakia.

# Chapter 20

# The Soviet Government's Decision in Early 1989 that Iskra Delta May Establish its Company in the Soviet Union

The establishment of a joint Yugoslav-Soviet company called TEDA, headquartered in Moscow near the Kremlin in the prestigious location of a building not far from the Soviet TASS agency and provided by the Soviet side, together with the initial capital needed to start the company, was worth several million U.S. dollars and was for those times incredibly quickly implemented, with immediate registration in the Soviet Union and Yugoslavia. The management board of TEDA was also quickly constituted and set about forming the management of the company. This joint company was to be in charge of technical cooperation and the early use of Iskra, especially Delta products, for the needs of the Soviet Union and Warsaw Pact countries. It was also supported by the members of the Soviet delegation to Slovenia who specifically requested to start the company as quickly as possible, saying it was important for further cooperation between Yugoslavia and the Soviet Union.

Today we know that the KGB gave the initiative for setting up the company. Its agents invited the leaders of Iskra Delta's field dealing with the East to an informal dinner in Moscow where they proposed, due to the better cooperation and the planned increase in sales of products and services for Iskra Delta in the East, a joint company as the most appropriate form of organization to provide long-term, mutually successful cooperation. This initiative was at that time even more unusual because until then the Soviet Union did not allow the establishment of such companies. It was, therefore, immediately clear that these Soviet representatives had broad powers and that the establishment of a joint company with Iskra Delta would be a major exception, so long as the latter agreed to it. This kind of company in the East had been the desire of the management of Iskra Delta for quite some time; therefore, the representatives accepted the Soviet proposal, and events began to take place incredibly quickly for Iskra Delta.

Even before the Soviet delegation's visit, Iskra Delta's exports to the Soviet Union and other countries in the East had risen exponentially, but immediately after the visit the orders escalated so much that the field responsible for sales in the East became by far the most successful of all. The sales managers for the East, based on the visit of the Soviet delegation, prepared a comprehensive strategy of approach to this market and in particular took into account the new sales opportunities provided through a joint company in the Soviet Union thus they led all activities relating to the creation of this company.

The ability to operate through a company, owned jointly, gave the Soviet Union new and larger dimensions and values that nobody in Iskra Delta dared to even consider before the visit. The business volume based on the demonstrated needs of the Soviet Union could reach an annual value of a hundred million U.S. dollars and more in sales in the Soviet Union within one to two years after the establishment of the joint company, as the products of Iskra Delta based on the business through a joint company would develop the characteristics of the domestic products.

Payments were provided for in convertible raw materials that could be offered by Iskra Delta through its business partners to Western convertible markets and earn more money. This is the way it had managed transactions with earlier customers of its equipment in the Soviet Union, and Iskra Delta had good experience with this method. Besides, the possibility of a new joint company with the Soviet Union oriented in business activity was something new; until then, their system did not allow establishment of such economic links. Therefore, it came as an even greater surprise in Iskra Delta when, after a formal request sent to the government of the Soviet Union to establish the joint company, all the necessary formalities were arranged within a month, after which the Soviets clearly showed that they placed immediate priority on the cooperation on the basis of Iskra Delta's achievements.

This rapid positive response impressed everybody in Yugoslavia and had a great echo throughout the public because, until then, very few foreign companies had their own business in the Soviet Union.

Just one week after receipt of the decision on the issued permit, representatives designated to participate in the business management of TEDA came from the Soviet Union to the Iskra Delta office in Ljubljana, where they immediately began discussions on the organization, stature, business, and development strategy, and the human resource aspects of who would care for the start of operations at the site the Soviet government had determined for the seat of the newly established company. It was planned that the director of the company would be from Ljubljana, and his deputy from Moscow. Because of the experiences that Iskra Delta had with their company in Austria, they were able to organize the steps to start the new business in Moscow relatively quickly. In all of this, Iskra Delta executives were led in particular by their interest in quickly reaching the desired business results, no matter what the specific conditions of working with the Eastern countries represented.

At that time, enthusiasm was fuelled by the huge potential of the conquest of the giant Eastern market. The Iskra Delta executives did not know the background of the resolute insistence by the Soviet representatives of why the joint company had to begin without delay, especially with the development and transfer of computer equipment production.

To gain time to inform the U.S. government and obtain the proper permits, they decided to start the production of a video terminal in the Soviet Union for the Eastern market. Iskra Delta had already completely mastered terminal production, and they did not contain components that would be under U.S. export control; therefore, no prior authorization from COCOM was needed, which greatly simplified the preparation of activities relating to the transfer of production. In the beginning, it was intended that all the parts for the first series would be assembled in the Soviet Union by Iskra Delta, and then they would gradually begin to replace the parts with those that could already be produced to a high quality standard by the Eastern Bloc countries.

The plan of cooperation with the Soviet Union was coordinated in the same way, by gradually organizing the production of other products by Iskra Delta in the Soviet Union and in other countries that were under Soviet influence. Regarding the division of work, they agreed to take into account the specialization already agreed between the Eastern countries on entering the field of manufacturing information technology products. Certain areas of production of computers and their peripherals had already been implemented in these countries, most of which were copies of old American models, notably IBM and DEC. These manufacturers had major problems with their production because of the complications in purchasing computer components put in place by the Western intelligence agencies, particularly the CIA. These components, which could not be replaced with their own, were urgently needed in the production of copies of U.S. computers, so they had to buy them on unfavourable terms in the West.

In Yugoslavia in early 1989, inflation hit its highest, at 100 percent, which caused enormous problems mainly for fast growing companies. Iskra Delta executives were not sufficiently aware of the possible external threats due to the sudden increased cooperation with the Soviet Bloc because they were busy trying to provide their own high quality money quickly for maintaining the company's liquidity due to the high costs caused by abnormally high inflation. They saw the solution to this situation in ever greater exports, particularly to the Eastern Bloc countries, where they achieved higher prices and, therefore, higher earnings. The results of this orientation were evident very quickly because they earned a lot of money selling to the Soviet Union and other Eastern Bloc countries, among which sales to the Poles stood out the most favourably. Because of this, the first quarter of the fiscal year 1989 was more successful than expected, as exports increased by more than 250 percent over the previous year, despite the galloping inflation in Yugoslavia at that time. Financial inflows from this market were becoming increasingly critical for normal operations.

This was also something that the KGB agents realized, so they began to blackmail the director of Iskra Delta by saying that the Soviet Union would regard Iskra Delta as a Western company and that the payments for already supplied computers would no longer be so easy if it did not abandon the request for consent from the Americans to cooperate with the companies of the Eastern Bloc. They requested that Iskra Delta, without the permission of the U.S. administration, begin immediate production of its computers in the Soviet Union. As this did not and would not happen, Soviet customers soon began to recite amended regulations, which did not entitle Iskra Delta to the payments for the already purchased computers within the agreed time.

In May of 1989, the debt from the East was already more than ten million dollars, and Iskra Delta found itself with its worst financial liquidity problems ever. An additional severe burden was caused by the unstoppable Yugoslav inflation and the high costs of expensive, short-term borrowing on the grey financial market to bridge the situation caused by sudden delays in payments from the Eastern market. Iskra Delta had previously succeeded in covering most costs from current operations, generated due to typically urgent investments in new product development and the conquest of new markets outside of Yugoslavia, but despite all its success in business and large market potential, in those critical moments, policy in Slovenia did not allow them to obtain appropriate long-term liquidity and investment funds from the banks.

Because of the increasingly rapid developments in information technologies, Iskra Delta, to at least keep up in the field, took the only possible option and took loans under very unfavourable conditions in the grey money market, which in this abnormal situation of rising inflation caused even greater liquidity problems, even to those who operated in such a rapidly evolving field. In such a tight liquidity situation, the management decided to immediately sell or mortgage facilities the company did not absolutely need for the business that were worth several million dollars, but even with this measure did not receive immediate support from the banks. Due to unforeseen financial problems caused by delayed payments for equipment already delivered to the Soviet Union, Iskra Delta was becoming increasingly dependent on the Iskra internal bank and on the Iskra management, who were not really in favour of Iskra Delta and its leadership.

The provision of operations liquidity strongly occupied the Iskra Delta management, which was always very much aware that this financial vulnerability could be taken advantage of by its enemies to carry out their plans. In the ever greater business anarchy that reigned in Yugoslavia at that time, and with higher inflation every month, the management had to spend most of its time selling opportunities to the East in order to save the company from its problems with the planned financial inflows. If regular payments had come as early and as clearly specified in the signed contracts, the problems would not have arisen. The optimistic outlook on the smooth cooperation in the beginning and then on the planned further development of the business with the East was further strengthened by the visiting Soviet delegation headed by President Gorbachev.

That Iskra Delta had started to rely too much on cooperation with the East was something that deeply concerned the Western agents, so they took advantage of the company's current financial difficulties and began to sow unrest among staff experts, using their own people inside Iskra Delta. This primarily took advantage of the fact that among some people dissatisfaction prevailed with the organizational changes necessary to adapt to rapidly changing conditions regarding the high potential in the Eastern markets. Further frustration was caused by not adjusting salaries fast enough due to the occasional lack of liquidity caused by the rampant inflation. Demands by employees to increase personal incomes were rising. At that time, payroll was guaranteed by law for employees on a particular day; this required major financial efforts for many companies to gather sufficient financial resources on their accounts on the day of payment.

Development and production companies were in a particularly difficult situation because of this, especially those with structures of highly educated professionals, as they had to provide adequate financial funding for higher amounts of money on every payment day every month. To reduce the debt on the grey market and coordinate the planned inflows of financial resources from the market with the payment of personal incomes, the director of Iskra Delta announced a lag in payment of salaries for a few days in May of 1989. Because of this, a group of workers in the manufacturing and development centre in Ljubljana, perhaps because of external influences, announced a suspension of work, which in former Yugoslavia was at the least unusual if salaries were not paid on the scheduled day.

Due to an error in the estimated position of the company, the director did not take the threat of work termination seriously and did not allow additional debts on the grey market. He was expecting the promised money from abroad in a few days for the already supplied computers. The director and his close associates were surprised by the work termination. At the Assembly of Workers, he tried to explain the

difficulties in which they found themselves due to high inflation and late payments from the East, but in that moment the
workers were much more interested in the timely payment
of their personal income than in development and the cause
as of the delay. Powerlessness to provide the timely payment
of salaries, and convinced that the obstacle to the provision
of bridging loans from the bank was himself, the director
decided to irrevocably resign as director at the next work's
council meeting. This move completely surprised many,
much more than the previous work termination.

In making this decision, he was not fully aware of the important role that Iskra Delta played between the enemies
during the Cold War, as he was unaware of its background
and the fact that information technology was crucial to the
outcome. Intelligence services were well aware that the ob-
struction of financial management was the only effective
means of putting pressure on him and on Iskra Delta to slow
its ambitious development. As such, he did not even suspect
why he got the invitation to the prestigious school in the U.S.
This dispelled his last doubts about the correctness of his decision and gave him extra strength to resign from the post of
director. The opponents in the Iskra leadership took advantage of this and vigorously and immediately instigated the
pre-prepared plan of liquidation of Iskra Delta, which was
something they succeeded in doing in a mere six months.

# Chapter 21

# The Destruction of Iskra Delta, Disintegration of the Soviet Union, and the End of the Cold War. The U.S. becomes the only World Power with the Means to Manage the World: the Dollar, IT, and the Military

The sudden decision of the director of Iskra Delta to resign and pursue additional education in the U.S. at the prestigious institute, the famous MIT (Massachusetts Institute of Technology), surprised everyone involved in what was happening around Iskra Delta, with the exception of those who had prepared the plan and rapidly put it into motion.

After the visit of the Soviet delegation headed by President Gorbachev and regarding the agreements reached on the transfer of production from Iskra Delta to the Soviet Union in the shortest time possible, American officials increased pressure on their colleagues in the republic's government and in the leadership of Iskra to stop the fulfilment of agreements between the Soviets and Iskra Delta. They used financial pressure and strategic misinformation among employees. Because of this, they were satisfied with the director's resignation. The director of Iskra Delta believed his resignation would prevent extortion by the Soviets in failing to make payments because he had not agreed to transfer the full Iskra Delta technology to the East without the agreement of the Americans. The Americans feared that Iskra Delta's technology would sooner or later come into possession of KGB agents, which is why they supported the enemies of Iskra Delta in Slovenia who had a plan for the liquidation and the selling off of its assets.

Opponents who had their own plans for Iskra Delta did not know the real cause of the director's sudden resignation and were especially pleased to get rid of one of the key creators and strategists of Iskra Delta's development policy, all in a very elegant and unexpected way, someone who they could not change after repeated failed attempts. Above all, the Iskra leadership, in agreement with some members of the republic's government, acted quickly and, through Iskra's internal bank, initiated activities for the prompt liquidation of the company, which at the time was becoming a recognized leader in Europe in the field of information technology and had more than 2000 employees, including more than 1000 professionals, and huge potential in the markets of the Soviet Union, China, and India.

With the cunning promise by the Iskra leadership that they would solve all current liquidity problems of Iskra Delta using their bank, they persuaded the temporary leadership of Iskra Delta, which they had set up themselves, and the workers' council for Iskra Delta, to transfer most of the assets to the Iskra internal bank.

In return, they received a promise to bridge the current financial liquidity problems, which were due to a combination of circumstances and internal problems at Iskra Delta. The unexpected resignation of the director, liquidity problems, and disagreements between the new executives at Iskra Delta resulted in the situation where the buyers soon began to hold their orders, which of course led to further deterioration in the liquidity situation and had an impact on Iskra Delta paying its bills to domestic and foreign suppliers, which further delayed the delivery of components. Everything began collapsing in a vicious circle.

Iskra Delta was also increasingly late with deliveries of already ordered computers, and this caused confusion not only for existing users, but also for future buyers. The situation was growing more difficult from month to month mainly because the Iskra bank intentionally, at the behest of the Iskra management, did not fulfil its promise to bridge the liquidity problems, so that eventually individual parts of Iskra Delta began to address the problems in their own ways. Due to its increasing problems, confusion, and the emerging panic among the employees, the temporary leadership also failed to set a successful recovery program to resolve the situation.

The pressure on the temporary leadership of Iskra Delta increased daily, as its opponents acted in unison, taking advantage of the situation in Yugoslavia, which was at that time driving toward utter chaos. Since the inter-republic work arrangements no longer applied, everybody was trying to save themselves as best they knew how. Because of discouragement and panic, which gradually overshadowed the managerial staff as well, everyone in Iskra Delta overlooked the already well-planned and agreed upon projects of sales to the East, causing restlessness and even panic among their partners in the East who relied on and were putting everything into Iskra Delta technology and their long-term cooperation.

Since the core of the battle took place in the background between the intelligence services, which only a few people knew then, the great business plans with the Soviet Union were also affected. Valid, already-signed contracts for tens of millions of dollars could not be fulfilled because the Soviet agents required that, before the Soviet customers pay for the already-supplied computer equipment, Iskra Delta had to transfer its technological achievements to the TEDA joint company without waiting for the appropriate permissions from the U.S. administration, which was something the Iskra Delta executives refused to do. On the other hand, the unexpected delay in payments from the Soviet Union led to financial problems for Iskra Delta, opening the door for the Iskra management and its internal bank to implement its plans in

collusion with covert U.S. agents' instructions for the liquidation of Iskra Delta to keep its technology out of the hands
of the Eastern agents in any way possible.

The players who led the background collapse were well
aware that they needed to stain Iskra Delta and its leadership
in public, so newspapers literally competed over who would
write the most fictional articles on events in Iskra Delta and
the alleged roguery of its leadership. The Iskra executives
began the immediate sale of its assets in both Austria and
Yugoslavia via their internal bank, and finally called for the
illegal bankruptcy of the company that, until a year before,
was among the best and most successful in Yugoslavia and
was the carrier of technological progress in the field of information technology to the Eastern countries.

Since the speed of this illegal declaration of bankruptcy
was important, the leadership of Iskra decided to appoint the
director of the Iskra bank himself as the liquidator, charging
him with the task to sell all the major assets of Iskra Delta
within six months and to first liquidate Iskra Delta's development department as fast as possible. They immediately fired
key development professionals, who would each take away
integral development knowledge and documentation, so that
no one person could continue an organized group of development projects within another organization. This liquidator
later claimed that he had to conduct the liquidation under
the threat of personal liability, and that his career was at stake
if the bankruptcy was not performed in the manner which
he was ordered by certain influential people in Iskra and the
republic.

It is interesting that the liquidation of Iskra Delta coin-
cided with the accelerated disintegration of Yugoslavia. As
both the Yugoslav and the republic's policy staff were especially busy with the battle for survival against the emerging
democratic processes, the rapid collapse of a very successful
company had not particularly disturbed anyone. Only with
the onset of the new authorities in the new state of Slovenia
were questions raised among the public: how was it possible

that the Iskra companies sank so quickly, Elektro optika, Mikroelektronika, and Iskra Delta, the companies that were working so successfully on future technologies?

To this end, a parliamentary commission was appointed in the mid-eighties out of public pressure and incentives by Iskra Delta delegates at the Assembly of the Republic of Slovenia to investigate the political responsibility of the government at the time for the collapse of these companies. This commission, of course, could not come to many correct conclusions, since the background of related events was not yet publicly known; for example how and with what funds the intelligence services of East and West in the Cold War conducted the battle with each other, and which officials of the government in Yugoslavia and especially in Slovenia were under the influence of certain foreign intelligence agencies or their agents.

The Commission knew even less, according to its composition, even the facts that during the Cold War between East and West there was a battle for technological supremacy in all strategic areas, and that in this struggle a major role was played by the latest developments in information technology, often developed by the most progressive Iskra companies, especially Iskra Delta, and that this was the key to why they all so mysteriously collapsed. In the early nineties when the Cold War finally ended, the U.S. administration lifted the embargo on exports of sophisticated technology products. This allowed huge profits primarily for their own companies, since they could then successfully operate even in markets that had been closed for them during the Cold War.

Shortly after the liquidation of Iskra Delta, major changes began in the Soviet Union due to economic and technological problems. It had become clear that their empire was unable to maintain its position in the Cold War and the arms race because of its underdeveloped economies. The Soviets under the leadership of Gorbachev sought to escape from this subordinate position with the introductions of Perestroika and Glasnost, trying to pull out with the introduction of democratic relations, but it was all too late. The Cold War had exhausted them so much economically that they were no longer able to handle such a state. Poorer nations under their control were becoming poorer, which resulted in unrest and led to the rapid disintegration of the empire into several independent states.

With the collapse of the Soviet empire and the emergence of several new independent states, the embargo on the export of computer technology was no longer necessary, as it had achieved its purpose and would soon primarily benefit U.S. companies who would seize the huge market that had previously been successfully managed by Iskra Delta and then disabled by Western intelligence services. These services made use of the chaotic collapse of Yugoslavia, and because the then-Yugoslav political leadership was busy in the struggle for power, they managed to liquidate the most dangerous competitor to their large Western information technology companies in the big Eastern market in that field.

With the collapse of the Soviet Union, the West opened a huge market in the East, so that their victory in the Cold War not only brought them unprecedented military and technological advantages, but also huge profits for their companies, especially for the U.S. companies whose products had already saturated the Western markets. In addition to conquering the huge market in the East, the most valuable developments for the U.S. in the Cold War were certainly the great progress in information technologies and, most importantly, the birth of the Internet.

The Cold War passed without direct military conflict, fought only by aggressively operating intelligence services of the countries that were involved. That is why the casualties were primarily just among the agents who worked on the ground in their foreign enemy countries. There would not have been such technological development in all fields without the Cold War and especially not in the field of information technologies on which the U.S. correctly relied. Of course, there would be one main product of this war, the

Internet. The Cold War resulted not only in the U.S. victory over the Soviet empire, but also in a crucial tool in the form of the Internet for effective management of the global world.

The U.S. also dominated the world with its dollar, which has become the only world currency trading in global raw materials and goods. It controls the global financial system, which is based on the dollar, and financial information systems, which are mainly active in the American computers and their communications equipment. This allows the U.S. to completely dominate the global flow of money and the debt of individual countries in a way that most countries do not even realize.

The U.S. dollar was introduced as the world currency at the height of the Cold War in the second half of the twentieth century, and this created the possibility to put into place a system in which the U.S. can owe itself in its own dollars, on proper authorization of the U.S. Congress. All other countries borrow from the American banks or from financial institutions under their control. With its military power and intelligence agencies, the U.S. ensures that trade takes place only in dollars for the most important raw materials, particularly oil.

Notwithstanding the fact that never again would there be such a cold war between the East and West, intelligence services still operate, as they still abide by the rule that *nations may be friendly but there are no friendly intelligence services*. Even at the height of the Cold War, the classic principle, *the enemy of my enemy is my friend*, was not always true because national interests always came first and still come first now, only now they are gaining new importance in the competition of economic interests.

Cultural and historical friendship between people of the world is a key to establishing trading partnerships. While those cultural and historical friendships between nations are still an important factor, the emerging trading partnerships and independent economic links have become a powerful force of global importance and are deeply dependent on military alliances. Independent of direct economic links, such military alliances are now primarily designed for the protection of economic partnerships.

The winners of the Cold War and conquerors of the global economy have entered into regional alliances to share information, and seek to raise the totals of their individual and collective economic power. In this way intelligence services are also given a new purpose and new, more modern tools to achieve the objectives and interests of their countries. For the Cold War winners, these tools bring new technologies for digital espionage and remote control of events on our planet. The traditional role of spies in obtaining, analyzing, and communicating classified information has been replaced by modes of operation that previously could not have even been imagined.

A satellite system has a very important role now; it allows, especially the U.S., who alone possesses the world's most advanced and powerful information technology, to digitally control and monitor events all over Earth in almost real time. This is made possible by the exponential progress in digital signal transmission and computer processing power, as these satellites can, in the role of spies in space, control events on Earth regardless of coverage by clouds or darkness in real time. Using infrared cameras, radar, and various delicate remote sensors, they can distinguish objects one centimetre in size and analyse them at the same time. The strategic role of satellites is tactically complemented by small, pilotless, flying robots, able to monitor a selected area of Earth for a number of days. There are always new ears being put into space, usually presented as weather or mapping satellites to the public, tapping all forms of communication signals that are transmitted into the ether.

Consciously accelerated use of wireless communications in phone calls and data transfer is effectively controlled using antennas mounted on satellites. The signals are then transferred to stations on Earth, where they are analyzed by means of very powerful and fast computers. Computer programs for speech recognition, designed for analysis of information systems, in combination with artificial intelligence systems which differentiate and filter unnecessary information to only relay the secrets that are communicated by either friends or enemies are crucial in the work of today's intelligence services. Faster computers allow especially the Americans to break even the most complex codes typically used in communications between intelligence agencies. One of their faster and more powerful computers, the IBM Blue Gene / L reaches speeds of over 280 teraflops (trillions of floating point calculations per second). This is several times faster than the fastest Japanese and European computers, which are further behind similar computers in the U.S. in numbers as well as speed.

Transforming the Internet into an information highway has radically changed ways of obtaining information; 90 percent of the information spies need they now find on the Internet. The Internet has become the world's library of knowledge and the main source of information needed in everyday competition of the world's economic superpowers. The key to its origin is easy access to the network, capability of the rapid exchange of information, and then using very powerful computers that are not sold commercially on the market to analyze the information, and thus reveal any hidden data or find useful information that could be important for subscribers in achieving their goals. Software applications experts play an important role in this, as one capable computer programmer is now able to find out more vital information in a single day than the classic spies could in their whole lives.

The Internet is also crucial in facilitating the transfer of secret information from spies to their superiors. It is precisely here in this final act that many were caught during the Cold War, no matter what the original means of communicating stolen information. With the help of the Internet, spies can now safely and within a few milliseconds send messages, information, and signals hidden in packets, which would previously have taken days or even months. Due to the exceptional opportunities offered by the use of the Internet to direct and control the events on Earth, the West still invests huge resources into its continuous improvement and thereby promotes and accelerates the introduction of its use in all aspects of life on our planet.

The initiatives for continuous improvements to the Internet and its standards, as well as requirements for even faster networks, mainly come from the USA. The Americans are only too aware that most people on Earth will be forced to use the next generation of the Internet in their lives, and that they will be able to effectively manage and monitor events on the planet only if the development and determination of its standards is in their hands. To this end and over the next few years of this century, the leading American universities, with relevant government projects and the support of large technology companies and government development projects, will finally manage to develop a new generation, Internet 2, also known as Video Internet, designed for the level of commercial use and which will initially be available only for professional and research work, not for widespread use. Video Internet will work on networks of optical fibres, which are increasingly being built, mostly in developed countries, and to which initially only selected users, such as the following, will be connected:

- Financial institutions (banks, insurance companies, etc.)
- Companies with e-commerce
- Suppliers of IT services and devices
- Publishing companies
- Export companies
- Manufacturers, retailers, and suppliers
- Construction companies
- Foreign global companies, their subsidiaries and resellers
- Educational and research institutions
- Hospitals and health care
- Government administrations

These users will be connected over the entire planet, from one end to the other, with optic cables that will enable them to communicate with each other in real time as if they were all together in the same room, even though they will actually be hundreds of miles apart.

The virtual elimination of physical distance in mutual contact will allow customers more time for active professional work and study, as there will no longer be any need for time-consuming and expensive travelling from place to place and from one meeting to another. But the biggest advantage of the development of a global optical network and the use of computer capabilities will be to enable users to work in the manner as is currently used in the electrical network (grid computing). The main development and power of the network will be with large computer facilities and databases, and the control over them will certainly be in the United States.

Therefore, only from the current time perspective is it possible to understand why the Americans were so shocked at the presentation by the director of Iskra Delta in Washington, where they realized that a small and unimportant Yugoslav company might break down their overall strategic plans if it was to develop in the direction it introduced in the presentation and was fuelled with the strategic development of the U.S. in the development of information technologies as basic raw materials for complex products of the next millennium. The planned development of Iskra Delta presented an objective threat to the interests of the United States of America; this reality was proved in 1985, at the time of the very origins of the Internet, when this company was able to build a similar foundation of its network over the entire territory of China, something the Americans refused to believe at the time of the presentation in Washington.

But the Americans soon realized that this company, formed by chance, of ambition, enterprise, courage, and the self-initiative of its experts, wanted to prove itself in a new field and believed in its vision for success. Knowing that Iskra Delta was not established with the support of former

Yugoslavia and that it did not have the support of Yugoslav policy, it was crucial that the Americans only observe Iskra Delta at first in its development, but only up to the time when the great powers, especially the Soviet Union, became interested in its achievements. The risk that the achievements of Iskra Delta would come into the hands of the KGB agents in Yugoslavia accounted for the very existence of this rapidly expanding company. Being in part a result of the battle for information technology as it was playing out during the Cold War, the company simply became too great a danger to American interests in the world.

Information technology has become an important commodity today, almost like water, and a very important driver of life on the planet. With its help, a long-term plan was made by the U.S. to win the important and so far the least bloody war, because the government supported its development at the right time through appropriate development projects at U.S. universities and institutes, while at the same time allowing for the arrival of the best brains from around the world to work at its development and educational institutions. With such support and a clear development strategy, these American institutions could be of the greatest help to society and contribute significantly to the development of its economic and military power, and on this basis, also bring victory in the Cold War.

This extraordinary support for the accelerated development of information technology in the U.S. universities has been continuous since the end of the Cold War. With such support, researchers at American universities can use the world's fastest computers in development projects that continue to be ordered by U.S. government agencies. These computers, for example, IBM's Big Red supercomputer, are not offered freely on the commercial markets. Big Red was installed recently at Indiana University and is, according to available information, the fastest in the academic environment in the world, with unprecedented computing speed of 20.4 trillion mathematical operations per second. It will enable the university to make new scientific discoveries in the shortest time possible.

What is interesting about this is that today's fastest supercomputers are based on the parallel processing of large numbers of processors, which is the same concept as Delta's PARSYS system presented by the Iskra Delta development experts at American universities as early as 1987. This confirms that Iskra Delta was on the right track in its strategic development, just in the wrong country at the wrong time. Also, the previously mentioned fastest computer in the world, the IBM Blue Gene, which is the result of joint development between IBM and NNSA (National Nuclear Security Administration) and is installed at Lawrence Livermore National Laboratory where it is primarily used to simulate nuclear weapons explosions using its dual core architecture and 131,072 processors, reaches a speed of 207.3 trillion floating point operations per second, making it by far the fastest among the five hundred supercomputers in the world, of which the vast majority are used in the United States.

Most of these supercomputers around the world use Linux operating software, which is used by ever more scientists and other demanding users worldwide due to its open architecture, which allows rapid development of its operating software and easy data exchange and programs via global optical infrastructure, which is also becoming ever faster.

Big Red also plays a major role in the TeraGrid project of the American Science Foundation (NSF) with the task of building a new cyber infrastructure for the development of next generation information technologies. Cyber infrastructure consists of supercomputers, massive data storage systems, very complex computer-controlled instruments, and leading scientists from different fields of development, all associated with a very fast optical network.

Implementation of this project will enable the United States to continue to be the leader in the world and to make even faster scientific discoveries with it, as well as realize the development of new, more demanding, and more complex technologies such as artificial intelligence, increased speed of memory, and the miniaturization of computers. The recently developed Intel hybrid laser will also greatly contribute and open a new chapter of development in building high-speed broadband computers.

Soon, all this will have an impact on the accelerated development and production of intelligent robots that will work with artificial consciousness and will be used as intelligent beings without emotions, in favour of their masters-operators. These intelligent artificial beings will soon replace workers in the most critical positions in factories and soldiers on the battlefield, and will have a major impact on our lives and living on our planet.

Information technology, for which the standards, development, and production of key components still continue to be dominated and defined by the United States, is becoming an increasingly crucial and indispensable tool in the development of life on Earth and, at the same time, the key to managing the world from one place of power. By controlling the development of information technology standards and promoting their use in all fields of work and life, the United States of America can manage the events on Earth and in space today, and even more so tomorrow, without serious competition, regardless of whether its inhabitants wish it or not.

# Epilogue

## The Cold War brought Development and Economic Recovery to the West and Disaster to the East

The Cold War, which began after the Second World War between the Soviet Union and the United States of America resulted in the armament race, where the Soviet Union basically invested tremendous resources to compensate for the technological gap they had with the U.S. In this respect, they resorted to all means, in particular to the theft of the American technology wherever this was possible. With the help of their spies in the U.S. they managed to achieve it. In a relatively short time, they came into possession of the technology for the manufacture of atomic bombs, which until then had represented the biggest advantage of the U.S. over the USSR.

When the Soviets successfully carried out a detonation of their first atomic bomb, it was a signal for the United States that it needed to prepare a new strategic weapons plan to maintain its advantage over the Soviet Union, which was becoming increasingly aggressive with its possession of atomic and later nuclear weapons. The government of the United States of America responded to the Soviet government challenge by deciding to accelerate the development of the then little-known field of computers and information technology and solutions.

The correct and timely national strategic direction of the United States, supported by relevant laws adopted by Congress to accelerate the development of information technologies at universities in the U.S., has, since the first nuclear test conducted by the Soviet Union, allowed the United States continuous rapid development and the leading role in the world. A particularly important measure in this development was the ARPANET project, which was designed at the request of the U.S. Army. The completion of this project enabled the implementation of the first computer network in the world and the real-time connection to all major U.S. development potentials for the fulfilment of national, defence, and development projects.

It also laid the foundations of new developments in communication technologies in the world, which later facilitated the development of the Internet. With this orientation, the United States of America had prepared an excellent basis for victory in the Cold War between the East and the West, which was fought and won mainly because the Soviet Union, in its great excitement to have the atomic bomb, neglected the development of information technologies for a critically long time. Once this was realized, it was already desperately behind the United States of America in this field. The American social system, which allowed free individual business initiative, further contributed to the fact that the development of these new technologies in the U.S. was even faster, since it allowed and encouraged competition in research and innovation among all players involved. This contributed to the invention of new products, for example the microchip, which was invented in 1972 by Robert Noyce, and it gave an important impetus in the development and expansion of electronic and information technology primarily in the United States.

This was followed by other important innovations, both in hardware and especially software, and in turn, by the rapid creation of new companies. In contrast, the Soviet model of central management and planning disabled all initiatives if they were not in accordance with the pre-arranged plan and approved by the party. And the most fatal for the East was that the Soviet leadership of the time, regardless of the warnings by their own experts, did not believe in the development of computer technology at the time, only in physical work and the power and abundance of its weapons.

The timely U.S. strategic policy in promoting the development of this new field enabled the rapid development of information technologies, especially in the seventies and eighties, which enabled it to not only have a decisive advantage in this strategic field, but also the beneficial social transformation into a new industry of knowledge on this basis. This industry contributed countless new jobs in all areas of the country's economic and social life, which significantly helped raise GDP and thus integrally transformed the very quality of life in the United States for its inhabitants.

With this orientation, the knowledge that an individual could suddenly become important, regardless of skin colour or origin, had an immediate positive effect on race relations, which by that time was becoming more and more strained every day. Information technology did not in itself create the many new jobs and new benefits, but it indirectly contributed to the start of development of new industries, services, and new materials that were no longer based only on the Earth's resources, but rather on the knowledge and innovation of its people.

Soon the innovators in these emerging new industries became increasingly rich and began to overtake those who worked in conventional industries with old technologies and working methods without the use of computers. This focus on education and accelerated investment in the development of information technologies increased the national wealth in the United States in a very short time by more than a thousand billion U.S. dollars, and thus enabled the relatively painless gradual restructuring of the American society.

As the fast-growing new businesses in the United States suddenly needed more and more young professionals, the war in Vietnam became all the more obstructive, so the U.S. government decided to withdraw from the war. This gave the impression of its defeat to the rest of the world, but in essence the withdrawal from this conflict prepared it to take the upper hand and win the Cold War, all the while advancing the technological and economic supremacy of the U.S., and later resulting in its world leading role.

Now it is possible to more thoroughly understand why U.S. President Reagan, during eighties when the American companies controlled more than 80 percent of the computer market in the world in this area, further exacerbated the situation on exporting information technology products to the East while simultaneously accelerating the manufacture of new weapons and systems on the basis of this technology, since it not only gained military advantage with this strategy but effectively destroyed its enemy economically.

Due to its poor strategy at that fateful time, the East did not have a sufficient number of its own-produced computers, and even these could not be used efficiently in its military systems or in economic and social applications. It had no chance to make up for lost time quickly because it could not buy modern computers legally due to the Western embargo. After finally acknowledging its mistake, the East, particularly the Soviet Union, due to its late recognition of the significance of information technology and its own products not being based on new expensive computers, was forced to import them illegally from the West or to steal and copy the old inferior American ones. Thus, by illegally purchasing very expensive older types of American computers, the East exhausted itself economically more and more and lost in the war with the West rather quickly.

The West, particularly the United States, according to the results from its blockade of the East, soon realized that rapid development of information technology could be decisive for winning the Cold War and that with even tougher obstacles to the export of these technologies to the East, it could win without direct military confrontation.

In the early nineties, the resulting economic gap between the East and the West was unsustainable for the people in the East, causing a gradual decline and then the collapse of the political system in the Soviet Union and, consequently, in all the Eastern Bloc countries, which soon collapsed with no major turmoil. This resulted in victory for the West and the end of the Cold War.

It can be concluded from these events that without the strong and timely guidance of the United States in the development of information technologies and development in all related areas, the U.S. and the West would not have won the Cold War then. It is likely that this war would have lasted much longer and perhaps ultimately led to a nuclear confrontation with catastrophic consequences for the further development of life on Earth.

It can also be concluded that information technology enabled a decisive technological leap which decided the victory because in other areas, the East competed successfully with the West and was in some areas (nuclear bombs, missiles, and leadership in space) even better.

This technological and, hence, economic gap based on information technology at the end of 1989 was analogous to comparing the rapid fire rifle with the bow and arrow, as it relates to how the whites in the United States defeated the native populations in the previous century.

Based on what was said and the facts of the actual events, it is possible to understand why Iskra Delta, after successfully implementing the only computer network without influence from the West throughout China, and after its presentation of the PARSYS parallel computers project, became a subject of interest overnight, and the principal target for intelligence services of the leading countries of the world. In this context, the Easterners saw the solution to their problems in Iskra Delta and its technological achievements, and the West saw a threat to its technological advantage over the East.

The existence of Iskra Delta probably represented an additional danger to the West, since it was known that the Soviet Union, India, and China, where Iskra Delta managed to prove itself with its projects, were clearly interested in deepening their cooperation with the company. Iskra Delta was immensely attractive to them precisely because of its rapid development and possession of important technologies and because it was a source through which these countries could access technologies relevant to their further development without the obstacles to U.S. technology. These countries, which were under a strict technology embargo, began to establish strategic contacts at the highest political levels of the Yugoslav state so they could quickly come to the Iskra Delta technology solutions where they saw a possible alternative solution to the Western embargo.

It might be too smug to say that the presidents of those countries who visited the then already collapsing Yugoslavia at the end of the eighties only did so because of the technological development, which was at that time the domain of Iskra Delta, and as a result of the difficulties in which they found themselves in their own development due to the U.S. technology embargo, yet such thinking is becoming more and more historically justified.

The Iskra Delta executives were not aware of this at the time, but they tried, with the appropriate policy, to make Iskra Delta an important bridge in the field of information technology between the East and the West. But they did not accurately assess the political situation in the world and were, therefore, not sufficiently aware of the scope and topical importance that information technology played in the Cold War and its further development for the economic and political relations as well. It simply knew that, for the intact development of the company, the most important strategy related to fair relations with the U.S. administration, as demonstrated in Washington when the Americans issued the licenses to Iskra Delta for the export of DEC Vax processors to fulfil the project in China. It was also clear that the developments made by Iskra Delta would not have been possible without good cooperation with the leading U.S. companies, which was tolerated by the U.S. administration due to its underestimation of Iskra Delta's ability to compete on its own with the U.S. companies in technological development.

Because of all this, Iskra Delta executives did not agree to the tempting offers from the Eastern countries to speed up an in-depth cooperation with them in the development and manufacture of information technology products based on technological solutions, which were primarily the result of development at Iskra Delta on the basis of the U.S. standards and permits. At the end of 1988 and in early 1989, activities by the Eastern intelligence services to obtain the technological achievements of Iskra Delta were at their maximum, as they intended to end the hopeless situation in the East just in time, when they finally realized that without computers and without the latest technology solutions of information technology, they could no longer compete successfully with the West, and particularly with the United States of America, which increasingly dictated the pace of developments in the world.

Therefore, the events around Iskra Delta happened at high speed; the East started to blackmail Iskra Delta most severely because, even with their tempting offers, they failed to convince the leadership of Iskra Delta to violate the agreements they had with the United States and transfer their technology solutions to the rapidly established joint company in the Soviet Union.

This did not leave Iskra Delta without fatal consequences for its very existence, and during the most critical time of the Cold War, it suddenly found itself in the crossfire between the two Blocs without the protection of its own country. Its opponents quickly seized upon the opportunity, and it was consequently forced into illegal bankruptcy within six months, a record for those times.

But all was not lost. The laid-off workers of Iskra Delta, with their innovation and creativity, succeeded in a short time in establishing more than one hundred new IT companies. They have become the carriers of the IT development in their environments, and because of their invaluable experiences and knowledge, they have also occupied important leadership positions in Slovenia as well as in countries that were formed in south-eastern Europe.

# Sources and References

1. The content of this book is based on personal experiences of the author.
2. Index of additional sources and references:

Anning, N., Melvern, L. and Hebditch, D., *Technobandits*. Boston, 1984.

Computer shopper: COLD WAR COMPUTING

*The Iskra Newsletter* No. 44 (14. 12. 1987)

Kurzweil, R., *The Age of Spiritual Machines. When Computers Exceed Human Intelligence*. New York: Penguin Books, 1999.

Moravec, H., *Robot. Mere Machine to Transcendent Mind*. Oxford University Press, 1999.

*PRAKSA, Yugoslav Journal of Informatics and AOP*, Belgrade, May 1988.

Železnikar, A. P., "Parsys Expeditions to the New Worlds" in *Informatica* 11:3:76–80.71

Železnikar, A. P., "On the Way to Information" v *Informatica* 11:1:4–1872